Blinded by Obsession

ANN EL-NEMR

Jan-Carol
Publishing, Inc

"every story needs a book"

Blinded by Obsession
Ann El-Nemr

Published September 2016
Little Creek Books
Imprint of Jan-Carol Publishing, Inc
All rights reserved
Copyright © 2016 by Ann El-Nemr
Book Cover Design: Tara Sizemore

ISBN: 978-1-945619-03-8
Library of Congress Control Number: 2016950677

You may contact the publisher:
Jan-Carol Publishing, Inc
PO Box 701
Johnson City, TN 37605
publisher@jancarolpublishing.com
jancarolpublishing.com

To all the people that thought they found the love of their life,
but only discovered heartbreak in the end.

Dear Readers

Blinded by Obsession is about the love you feel (or should I say imagine) another person has for you, only to realize it was a one-way street and have your entire world shattered when you discover the truth. This story is about when you first fall in love, and you conjure feelings that are not reciprocated. In this novel, Rodney was happy just to watch Lucy from afar, until he became aware of another man who was trying to steal her away from him. He could not let that happen; he needed her—he desired her, and he loved her so much he would do anything to keep her. She belonged to him. A love triangle developed, and, as always, it doesn't end as you'd think it would. One person, or sometimes two, get hurt from the last decision made by one party.

It took me a long time to write this story, since I wanted an ending where every character was content. However, as you might know if you have read my other novels, I like to introduce a little drama and suspense into my characters' lives. The conclusion of this book is unexpected, due to one character's reaction to loss. I love to share my storylines as I'm writing and solicit opinions from my friends. It is a great way to gauge their enthusiasm for my story, as I twist it around to my satisfaction without ever telling them the ending. I hope you have fun reading my latest creation while sitting at the edge of your seat. Enjoy!

Yours truly,
Ann El-Nemr

Acknowledgments

I would like to express my gratitude to Mary Ong, from the bottom of my heart, for her eagerness and interest in my writing. She listens to me talk about ideas and scenarios of what should or could happen in my novels without criticism. She continuously has words of encouragement for concepts and schemes in my books. She is one of the first to know how I'm about to spin my plots, without giving her my final thoughts. Each morning, her laughter brings me joy. I love you, Mary. Thanks!

Introduction

Just a final thought to tell you I love to hear from my readers, and hope you will continue to support me as I go forward in my storytelling. I do it to entertain you, but most of all to bring you to another world where love is present and you can forget your troubles for just a short time. Make no mistakes, my stories always have a twist, because in life there are conflicts—and occasionally it doesn't end the way you thought it would. As long as I have fans who love to read my tales and are delighted, I will write them. It is by far the best hobby ever.

Chapter 1

It was eight o'clock on Saturday night. Lucy sat at the bar alone, on one of the many leather stools at Abe & Louie's, one of the many high-end, elegant steakhouses in Boston. She'd handpicked this restaurant because of the atmosphere; it was loud, busy and always filled with lots of people. Dark mahogany panels lined the walls. The white tablecloths glistened with fine crystal and delicate china adorned the tables. Waiters dressed in black were practically running back and forth, catering to all their customer's needs.

She wanted to hide among the patrons where no one knew her: where no one would bother her with questions about her life. She just wanted to enjoy a nice meal. She watched the people around her laugh and hug each other as they drank their snazzy cocktails and whiskeys—Blue Label Johnny Walker, of course. She shifted her weight in her seat. Suddenly Lucy didn't feel well; a chill ran down her back. Now she was sorry she had come out. Thoughts of her husband invaded her mind, like they did so many evenings when she was by herself and feeling lonely.

Two years ago, after a long police investigation, warrants, and endless pursuits, the police had killed her husband in a shoot-out after he murdered one of his colleagues. They had been in love for so many years, until that tragic day. It had all come to a head after he lost his company due to his fraudulent business methods, and was caught in his financial dealings. He had embezzled millions of dollars from his partners in an investment fraud scheme, and then he had tried to flee the country. One of his partners gave him up in a plea deal with the prosecution, and the authorities were alerted.

She was so naïve and gullible that she had never questioned his transactions during the whole time they had been married. She'd thought he could do no harm or anything illegal. Wow, was she wrong! Lucy wasn't charged with any criminal acts because she was never involved in his business—and she had been grateful to him for that. There was a long examination of evidence by the FBI; fortunately she was cleared of any wrongdoing, but her name had been smeared in the community of the investment department.

Even after all was said and done, she had been blessed with good luck; she'd been able to collect an insurance policy of millions of dollars after his death. She was now financially secure, but she had lost friends and business associates who didn't believe she was innocent. Lucy felt ashamed, an outcast even though she was blameless. People had labeled her with her husband. She shuddered at the thought as she relived the events over and over in her mind. Tears filled her eyes. She shook her head, trying to focus on where she was and what she wanted. She turned her head from right to left, examining her surroundings, wondering how she had ended up where she was in her life.

She lost her appetite immediately; her untouched filet mignon and salad stared at her. Lucy pushed her plate away with the tips of her fingers. She reached over to play with her crystal wine glass and observed once again the other patrons, eating and chuckling behind her, in the reflection of the mirror across from her.

Today was her thirty-fifth birthday. She was in a room full of people, yet she was filled with loneliness. *Why did I think going out to dinner alone to celebrate my birthday would cheer me up?* she thought. She lowered her head, wondering if anyone was watching her and if she would ever feel the fulfillment of happiness again.

Ten years ago, she'd moved to Boston from a small country town in Maine called Houlton, where people are simple, friendly, and unpretentious. A small rural area a few miles outside the Canadian border, it is the last stop before Canada on 95 North. Lucy had put herself through college at the University of Southern Maine while working as a waitress in a local restaurant in Portland, and tutoring other students at night. She earned an art degree, she struggled with money for years—until she met her husband at the art gallery where she was working in downtown Boston, eight years ago. *What a mistake that was! I need a new start where no one knows me; but where?* she thought. She motioned to the bartender to bring her check. He nodded her way. She took her wallet out of her bag and gave him her American Express credit card. Moments later, she signed her bill and pushed her chair away from the counter.

Lucy walked to the front door of the restaurant and stepped out into the fresh summer air. It was still early in the evening, and the streets were bustling with people of all ages strolling by her as she headed towards her car. She opened the door to her SUV and sat behind the wheel. Tears pooled in her eyes once again; she tried to blink them away, but it was no use. She covered her face with her hands and sobbed loudly. She needed to find a more tranquil lifestyle somewhere else, where no one knew her. She finally stopped crying after about ten minutes, wiped her eyes with the palms of her hands, and composed herself with a few deep breaths. She turned the key to start her Range Rover, and drove home in silence.

She unlocked her apartment door, dropping her handbag on the floor by the entrance. With a slow pace, she went to the kitchen and flopped down on one of the stool at the counter. Lucy glanced around her place of residence.

"What is keeping you here?" she asked herself out loud. She had nothing that tied her down: no job, no relationship, only a couple of friends...and she was miserable living as she was now. She had no desire to stay here, no future in this city anymore. Lucy was alone and wanted a fresh start, in a place where nobody knew what had happened to her. At that moment, she made the decision to return to her hometown. She got up, walked to her bedroom, and went to bed.

The next day, Lucy woke up rejuvenated. As soon as she opened her eyes, she stretched her arms in the air and immediately sat on the edge of her bed. Today she had a purpose, for once; she hadn't had one in a long time, and she was ready to make her move. She walked to the kitchen and made a cup of coffee, then picked up her phone. She dialed her landlord's phone number as she sipped her drink at the kitchen counter. She gave him a month's notice, and told him she would pay her last month's rent in person. She grabbed the phone book and leafed through it to hire a moving company. She was determined to start a new life back in Maine. There was nothing to keep her in Boston; she had money and would be able to live comfortably in this small town. Maybe, just maybe, she would meet someone to love again.

Within a week, workers had packed her furniture and stored it away in a local storage unit. She was on her way toward Maine, to a two-bedroom bungalow on the water that she found online. She'd rented it without even seeing the inside of it, and she'd signed a lease for a whole year.

She stood at the entrance of her apartment, looking at the empty rooms for the last time. She reached for the doorknob and held it tight, reflecting on her life for a minute. Then without hesitation, she closed the door behind her. She walked to her car, slid inside, turned the ignition, and drove away feeling lighter, leaving the past behind. She headed north on highway 95. Lucy put her tunes on loud and smiled to herself as she sang driving down the highway. She was excited about going forward with her new beginning.

The bungalow Lucy had found listed online was located on a lake in New Limerick, five minutes from Houlton. She had been driving her Range Rover for about six hours When she realized she was tired. The muscles in her neck and shoulders were starting to stiffen up from lack of movement. She rubbed her neck with her hand, but got no relief. *You're almost there; maybe a half hour at the most,* she thought to herself. She focused on the road, driving a little faster than usual and not paying attention to the speed limits.

Suddenly, she heard a siren. She glanced in her rearview mirror. A Maine State Trooper in his light blue car, blue lights flashing was right behind her. "Where the hell did you come from?" she said out loud. She turned down the music.

"Shit!" she said. Lucy looked at the odometer: eighty miles per hour. She was driving well over the speed limit. She released the gas pedal and started to pull over onto the side of the road. Lucy stopped in the breakdown lane and shut off the engine.. She grabbed her wallet from the passenger seat. She took out her driver's license, her auto registration, and insurance card.. She waited impatiently, tapping her fingers on the steering wheel. She watched for the state trooper in the side mirror without moving her head. The trooper opened his door and walked toward her. *Hmmm! Nice looking! He's looking even finer in his uniform,* she thought. She pushed the button to lower her window as he approached. *Why is my heart racing?* she asked herself. *Relax! It's only a ticket.*

"Good afternoon, driver's license and registration please," he told her politely as he looked briefly at her. He was gorgeous! He was tanned and tall, with a muscular body and high cheekbones—but she couldn't see his eyes behind the black shades. She squinted at him as she ogled. An inner voice in her head screamed, *Stop it!* She turned her head to look straight ahead, her face feeling hot.

"Where are you going in such a hurry? I clocked you doing over eighty. The speed limit in Maine is seventy," he said in a serious tone as he checked out the backseat. It was filled with boxes of her clothes and personal items.

"I'm sorry. I didn't notice I was driving that fast. I rented a house in New Limerick, so I was trying to get there as soon as possible, before dark. I have been driving since this morning and..." she replied, then noticed he was eyeing her and grinning at her. Lucy passed him the paperwork through the open window without another word. She looked straight ahead, because she had a feeling she was blushing. She could feel the heat rising up to her ears. *Oh, God! I'm beet red*, she thought, as she glanced at her face in the mirror.

"I'll be right back," he answered, and walked back to his squad car. She couldn't help, but notice his tight butt as he strolled away. Her eyes were glued to her mirror as she observed his every move. A few minutes passed as she watched him, intrigued. She wished he'd take his glasses off. *Here he comes!* Lucy sat up straight with her hands on her lap and waited for him to approach her SUV.

"Miss Marvin, I just gave you a warning for today. You need to slow down, especially in these parts. There's a lot of wild animals that cross the road. If you have any questions, the number here will help you. Have a nice day," he told her, pointing to the information number. He handed Lucy the warning ticket and her papers.

His fingers brushed against hers; she looked up at him and said, "Thank you, Officer. I'll make sure to be on the lookout for the creatures in the road."

He nodded at her, and then he did the most amazing thing; He gave her a broad smile. It took her breath away. He turned around and walked back to his patrol car. Lucy sat motionless, stunned. *Wow! I wonder if I'll ever see him again? What are the chances? Almost zero. Not likely.* She saw the squad car pull away from the curb and continue down the road. She should have said something, but what? *Excuse me, officer, could I have your phone number? I love the way you look in your uniform. Yes, that would work.* She giggled loudly and continued on her way to her new home.

***

Cole Baker had been a trooper ever since he graduated from the academy. It was what he loved to do, and what he had always wanted to do in life. He had been assigned to the Houlton barracks area for the last five years. He'd stopped thousands of drivers over the years, but the woman who sat twenty feet away in the Range Rover in front of him had taken hold of him. The minute he laid eyes on her, she fascinated him. He felt a sexual feeling surge; it wasn't something that often happened when he was on duty. *She is gorgeous!* he thought. There was something about red-haired women with green eyes that drove him crazy. Her fair skin, the freckles on her nose and cheeks...he loved those in a woman. He rarely encountered one he wanted to ask out, but he had to let this one go. It wasn't ethical. He raked his hand through his hair in defeat.

He sat in his cruiser, her driver's license in his hand reading the information. She was five feet eight inches, thirty-five years old; the address on her permit said she came from the Boston area. He glanced toward the vehicle. He noted she was watching him in her rearview mirror. He didn't want to write her up, so a warning was in order. He was glad she was going to be in the area. Maybe he would bump into her again. He hoped so! His mind wandered; how nice it would be, to have someone by his side. Cole had been alone too long. He needed to feel desired and wanted. He yearned for someone to fall in love with. He'd spent enough nights by himself. He would have to check out the New Limerick area a little more often, maybe! *Be professional, for God Sake! You can't go there looking for her*, he thought to himself. He grabbed his pen from his shirt pocket and picked up the ticket book by his side to issue her a warning citation. He made sure his penmanship was clear, so she could read his name.

He opened his door and within a few strides, he was standing next to her again. He could smell her perfume from where she sat. He couldn't keep his hand from touching hers when he passed her the citation. *Her skin is so silky*

6

and soft! Cole wanted to laugh when she gave him the reply about the creatures in the road, but instead he turned around and went back to his car. He slipped into his seat and took one last look in her direction. *Why didn't I ask her to go out for coffee? She probably would have refused anyway*, he thought. It was too late now. He started his patrol car, switched off the lights, and slowly pulled away.

That afternoon was like any other ordinary day—except he couldn't stop thinking of that woman, Lucy Marvin. The vision of her red hair and her floral scent were permanently engraved in his mind. He really wanted to see her again.

It was business as usual for him. He gave ten more citations and attended a motor vehicle accident. The day was coming to an end. The sun had gone down, and the stars were out in the sky. Cole had been so busy with his work he'd forgotten to grab a bite to eat earlier. His shift was over, so he hurried home to shower, and change into a black button-down shirt and jeans. He picked up his keys from the hook by the door and headed outside. He hopped on his black Harley Davidson, which was parked in the driveway, strapped on his helmet and rode down toward the town.

He decided to go to supper at the Ma and Pop Diner, not too far down the road from his house. He usually frequented the diner because it was so close to his home. It was owned and managed by a sweet older woman named Christy. She and her family had operated the eatery for the last twenty years. Her husband had died a few years back, so her oldest son, Harry, helped her. He was a good-hearted, potbellied man in his forties who had never married and had a heart of gold. He handled the front service with a part-time girl, while Christy made the delicious homemade meals in the back. Cole knew he could get a good home-cooked meal anytime day or night, and since he was a single man who didn't cook much, it was the perfect place when he was hungry.

The small diner only held eight worn leather booths, supplemented with a small counter big enough for six stools. It was a simple place, with blue-and-white checkered curtains and old pictures of the town on the walls. The food was to die for, and the service was always friendly. They mostly had locals because it was the last building on a dead-end street, so tourists rarely ventured down this way.

Cole parked his bike in front of the white-shingled building where a red sign flashed *open* in the window. He took the few steps to the glass door and entered. He walked into the restaurant to the last booth and slid in. Within minutes, Harry came forward to greet him, with a menu and water in hand. They had been friends for years.

"I don't need a menu, Harry. I'll have whatever your mother has for the day's special," Cole said. He removed his helmet and placed it on the seat, along with a newspaper.

"Good evening, Cole. The special is chicken pot pie, with potatoes and a vegetable. Is that okay?" Harry asked him and placed the glass of water in front of him.

"That's perfect! I'm starving," he answered as he gulped down the water.

The diner wasn't busy; no one else was there except for a few teenagers having burgers three booths down. Cole picked up his newspaper, opened it, and began to read the sports section.

Ten minutes went by when he heard an unmistakable voice. It was a voice he couldn't get out of his mind from earlier that afternoon. He brought down his paper a bit to peek over it and froze. It was her! A sexual urge came upon him when he saw the red-haired woman. She was sitting down on one of the stools at the end of the counter, about thirty feet away. She looked at a menu briefly, then ordered a meal from Harry. Cole folded his newspaper and placed it on the table.

He put his elbow on the table, resting his chin on his hand. Cole observed her every move; he watched as she pushed her hair from her face and bit her lower lip while she read the menu. She hadn't seen him yet, since she was busy deciding on her order. He tilted his head, keeping his eyes pinned on her. She sat on the stool fidgeting, watching as Harry walked to the kitchen to place her order. She looked around the place as if she had been here before. She crossed her legs then pivoted on her stool as she held her bag on her knees. She turned her head toward him; her mouth opened and her eyes widened when she spotted Cole, but no words came out. She nodded, then smiled his way. *Say something, you fool*, he thought.

"So, did you encounter any creatures on the road since I last saw you?" Cole asked. He sat up straight in his seat with his back against the booth.

Lucy giggled and glanced away for a second then looked straight into his eyes.

"As a matter of fact, yes, I did," she answered, but did not move from her spot.

"Why don't you join me, and tell me about it?" he laughed and motioned for her to sit across from him. She strolled over to his booth and sat down. He watched her hips swing smoothly from side to side and glide into the seat. She placed her hands in front of her on the table and gave him a wide smile.

"Well, I lied. I only saw squirrels darting across the road. You know, there are quite a few of those critters roaming the streets," she said and looked out the window. She blushed, and her face was all pink. Cole sniggered quietly.

"Good thing you didn't run them over. I would have had to write you up a ticket for endangerment," he answered her, poker-faced.

"Really!" she replied surprised.

He nodded seriously. However, he couldn't keep a straight face any longer, he burst out laughing. She did too, and shook her head.

"My name is Cole Baker," he said then extended his hand to her. She grasped it firmly and shook it. Her touch made him shiver from excitement. Her skin was so soft and delicate. No one had ever made him feel that way before now.

"I'm Lucy Marvin. I suppose you already know that," she replied quietly. She seemed a bit embarrassed as she cast her green eyes away from him and looked down at her hands, still resting on the top of the table.

"Yes, I remember." Not taking his eyes off of her face, Cole asked, "How do you know this place? It seems out of the ordinary."

"I was raised in Houlton. I used to come here when I was younger. Are you from around here?" she questioned him. She started to play with her long auburn hair nervously, twirling it between her fingers.

"No, I'm from the Bangor area. I've been stationed here at the state trooper office for the last five years. So, where are you leasing your home?" he asked her. Cole saw Harry coming forward with his meal and bread. Harry placed the dishes in front of him.

"Your take-out order should be ready any minute, Miss," he politely informed Lucy.

"Thank you. I'll leave you to your supper, Cole. It was nice chatting with you," she said, rising from her seat.

"Why don't you eat with me?" he asked, hoping she would agree. "I'm by myself, and would love the company. That is, if you want too." he asked, hoping she would agree. Cole wanted to know more about her. He didn't want her to leave, not just yet. He reached over and touched her arm lightly. How velvety it was! He wondered if her whole body was like that. *Stop it! Concentrate,* he thought and pulled his hand away.

"Sure, I'd love too. If you don't mind I'll eat inside," she told Harry. Harry nodded and smiled at her.

"Good, I hate eating alone, and I'd rather have a gorgeous woman by my side keeping me company anytime," he told her. She giggled a bit, then looked down at his plate.

"Go ahead. Please eat. Your food will get cold," she said, pointing at his plate.

"I'll wait for your meal to arrive; mine's too hot anyway. It shouldn't be long. I can wait," he lied. His stomach growled. He reached over, buttered two rolls, and handed her one. She took it, bit into it and chewed quietly.

"So, tell me, what made you move back? I think I'll order a beer. Would you like one?" he asked. He needed a beer to extinguish the fire that was burning in his groin. He desperately wanted to run his hands through her hair, pull her against his body and ravish her. He got a whiff of her fragrance again that engulfed his whole being. *How can a woman's scent smell so good?* he wondered.

Lucy silently nodded.

"Harry, could you bring us two Bud Lights when you come back this way?" he yelled.

"Sure, no problem. Coming right up," Harry answered, and grabbed two beers from the fridge.

"I just needed a change," she answered as she closed her eyes momentarily. Cole noticed she suddenly seemed sad as she bowed her head, and became tranquil as if she was thinking of someone.

"How's the house you rented?" He decided to change the subject, hoping she would cheer up.

"The house... Well, it looked a lot better in the pictures on the internet than when I saw it in real life," she told him. Cole wasn't sure if he should ask her about her whereabouts; he didn't know her. She might think it was too forward of him, so he kept silent. Harry was back, with their beers and her meal: *Thank God!* He was famished. She grasped her beer and took a sip, Cole immediately took a sip of his beer, too. He picked up his fork, dug into his pie, and took a mouthful of food.

"Why? What's wrong with it?" he inquired as he munched on his food.

"I think it will need a little fixing up, like painting. The porch needs a few boards replaced, among other things. Otherwise, I like it. It's peaceful and private," she said, then she began to eat her meal.

"I can help you with it, if you want. I have a toolbox, and I'm a pretty good handyman when I apply myself—no charge," he offered without hesitation. He really wanted to spend more time with her, and this gave him his opportunity.

"Sure, that would be great," she answered with a smile.

They talked for another hour, and had another beer each. Harry brought their check to the table. She instantly snatched it from him and pulled two twenties from her purse. She laid the money on the table, on top of the check.

"Since you're going to help me with the house and you won't let me pay you, it's the least I can do," she told him.

"Okay, I'm not going to argue. You don't even know how my work will be," he snickered as he stood up. They both got ready to leave the diner.

"Thank you for an enjoyable evening," he told her as they walked out of the diner to her car. He really wanted to kiss her. He had stared at her full lips all through supper, and when she licked them, he wanted to lunge at her. He opened the door of her SUV and she got in. Lucy took a pen and a piece of paper from her bag, then wrote down her phone number.

"Call me when you are free to do the work," she told him softly, and handed him her number. He took the small piece of paper and placed it in his front pocket, carefully.

"I'll call you tomorrow to make arrangements. Good night!" he said to her.

Lucy gave him one last smile, closed the door, and started the SUV. Cole took a step to the side to get out of her way. He watched as she backed out of the parking lot. He waved goodbye to her until he couldn't see her anymore. He walked over to his bike, wishing he was leaving with her.

Chapter 2

Lucy was in her own little world. She couldn't stop smiling all the way home; just thinking about Cole made her body hot with desire. She tapped the steering wheel to the beat of the songs on the radio as she drove back to her newfound home on Drews Lake Road. What a delightful surprise to meet the trooper she had leered at this afternoon. He'd even offered to help her with the renovations. *How considerate!* she thought. She would see him again. Maybe he was the one she had been looking for to bring her happiness. She sure hoped she was right.

She took a right onto a dirt road and drove up half-mile driveway to her bungalow; or she would call it a cabin. She had left the outside light on so she could get used to the terrain. She parked her SUV, then stepped upon the front veranda, and she took her key out of her purse. She inserted it into the lock, turned the key and entered.

Lucy loved the warmth of the house, and its open concept. The walls were pine, and large trunks formed the support beams. The furniture was rustic, but she didn't mind. It only had two bedrooms and one bathroom, but it had a large kitchen. She had a gazebo out back where she could relax and read while enjoying the view of the lake. It was charming, with a stone fireplace that would be handy during the chilly nights.

She closed the door behind her, then admired the view through the large windows that overlooked Nickerson Lake. One of the reasons she leased the place was because she had access to the water. She loved being away from people and not having neighbors right next to her. Lucy threw her bag on the kitchen table and walked to her bathroom. She turned the hot water on in the tub, and dropped a handful of bath salts into it. She decided to take a bath because it would help her fall asleep; she hoped she'd sleep well, since this was her first night. It would relax her tired bones from the long drive. She undressed quickly, letting the clothes fall where they may. She lit a few candles, found some country tunes on the radio, and stepped into the hot water; it engulfed her body in relaxation. She rested her head against the rim of the tub, put her feet up on the side, and closed her eyes.

Twenty minutes later, still soaking her tired body in the water, she was startled by a noise outside her bathroom window. Lucy sat up and turned toward the sound. Her eyes darted from left to right. She couldn't see anything; the curtain was closed. There was nothing. It became quiet again. *You're imagining things. It's probably a raccoon in that garbage can that's up against the wall, she thought to herself. Lucy, you're in the woods, for God's sake!* She felt was just being paranoid. *I'll have to make sure the lid fits tightly, so animals can't get into it.* "This is the country, not the city; calm down," she said to herself out loud.

An hour and several water warm-ups later, she finally left the tub and dried herself off. She then slipped on a pink cotton nightgown and was soon under the covers of her bed. Her mind was still on Cole. She closed her eyes and touched her lips with her finger, wondering how it would feel to be kissed by him. She rolled over onto her side and fell asleep quickly, with a smile on her face.

The rays of the sun beamed directly on Lucy's face the next morning. She squinted as she tried to open her eyes. She pushed the blanket away and sat up, yawning. Lucy stretched as she looked around the bedroom, and noticed the last box of clothes she hadn't gotten to do yesterday. She grabbed her robe, which was on the bed next to her, rose and headed for the kitchen. As she approached, she could smell the coffee brewing; she had put it on a timer the previous night. She poured a cup of java, added cream, then carried it to the front porch where she sat on the top step. She took a deep breath and smelled the fresh air. She gazed at the lake, listened to the birds chirping and smelled the clean air of the country. It made her happy that she moved away from the city. It was so peaceful! She took another sip and tilted her head back, so the sun could warm her face. She sat on the step while finishing her drink, just delighting in her view. Suddenly, she was startled by the phone ringing—but she didn't want to talk to anyone yet, or to disturb her perfect moment. She decided to let it ring. *Whoever it is can wait*, she thought.

Half an hour later, she stood up and walked back inside to put on something appropriate to go into town. The landlord had given her permission to fix and paint the deck, so that was what she was going to do today. Lucy threw on a pair of jean shorts and a T-shirt. She brushed her hair quickly, then put it up in a ponytail. She grabbed her bag and headed toward her truck, intending to go to town and pick up painting supplies. She was halfway up her driveway when she saw a black Jeep coming toward her. *Who could that be?* Lucy slowed to a stop parallel to him in the street, waiting; she had recognized the driver. It was *him!* Her heartbeat accelerated, and she pushed the button to bring down her window.

"Hi. What are you doing here? How did you find me?" Lucy asked, pleased to see him. She stared at him while holding on to the steering wheel tightly.

"Good morning. I tried calling you earlier, but you didn't answer, so I decided to surprise you. It's my day off today, so I thought you'd like to get your porch fixed as soon as possible. I picked up a few supplies, and I brought my tools," Cole answered. He pointed to his back seat and grinned at her. Her mouth opened, hung there for a second, then closed. Lucy was unable to speak for a moment, until she realized he was there to help her.

"You didn't have to... I didn't mean you had to do it the next day. I was just now going to town to pick up supplies," she replied, stunned.

"I'm sorry; if you have other plans I can come back later, or—" he said.

She interrupted him before he could finish his sentence. "No, no. I was just on my way to town; it can wait. Go ahead. I'll meet you at the house," she smiled at him.

"Are you sure?" he asked. She nodded affirmatively right away.

"Okay," he said, and drove up the road toward the bungalow. She made a U-turn and followed him. By the time she caught up with Cole, he had parked his jeep and was unloading his things from the backseat. *Nice body!* Lucy thought to herself once again, as she pulled in beside his Jeep. He wore a tight blue T-shirt that clearly showed the outline of his upper body muscles, beige cargo shorts, and hiking boots. Lucy loved the cap he was wearing; it had a Red Sox logo on the front—her favorite team. She got out of her car and walked over to give him a hand.

"That's okay, I've got it. I don't have much," he told her. He carried the two by four over and dropped it besides the veranda. Lucy couldn't keep her eyes off him as he pulled out a tool belt and attached it to his waist. She sat down on the top step, at a loss for words as he continued to get ready.

"Now, can you show me what needs to be fixed?" Cole asked. He stood in front of her with his hands on his hips, his cap turned backward. She raised her eyebrows at him, and she couldn't stop herself. Lucy chuckled at him. She placed her hand in front of her mouth and started to giggle, amused at how serious he was.

"What's so funny?" he asked baffled, waiting for an answer. Lucy motioned for him to sit down beside her with her hand as she suppressed another giggle and she tried to regain her composure.

"Slow down, please. First, how did you find me? I only gave you my phone number," she asked as he moved to sit beside her. His thigh touched hers as he sat close to her. She sucked in her breath from the contact. It didn't deter Cole; his leg didn't budge.

"Well, there is only so many places around here that were for lease, so I took a chance and drove here. It *is* a small town, and you mentioned you were located on the lake, so here I am," he told her. He clapped his hands together as he gave her a wide smile.

"You are some detective, I must say. Come on, then. I'll show you what needs to be replaced on the porch," she said and stood up. Lucy took a few steps and pointed to the floor. He came and stood beside her. Three floor boards needed replacement, since they were broken into two pieces.

"That's it? It won't take too much time," he replied, and looked out toward the lake.

"Great! Would you like an iced coffee? I'm thirsty! I'll leave you to get to it, and go make a pot while you repair the three boards. I'll be right back," she told him and pranced toward the kitchen door. Cole just stood there, shaking his head and grinning. Lucy realized she hadn't even waited for him to answer. She glanced back at him through the screen door just as he started to whistle a tune. He knelt down and unhooked the hammer from his belt to take out the rotten timber.

***

Cole was excited when he drove up the driveway and saw her coming toward him. He had gone to the hardware store early to buy planks and nails. He couldn't wait to see her again, so he took it upon himself to use fixing her porch as his excuse. He'd gathered his tools from his garage and placed them in the backseat. He had thought of Lucy all evening after they'd parted at the diner. He knew the lake area, so he figured it would be easy to find her—especially since there was only one main road to the lake.

Sitting beside her on the steps of her veranda, Cole could feel her soft thigh rubbing against his. He was glad when Lucy stood up to show him the work, because he really wanted to wrap his arms around her and kiss her: sure to be a disaster so soon after their first meeting. Being so close to her, he could smell her floral fragrance.

Cole ripped the nails out of the boards with the claw of his hammer. He threw the old ones over the railing in a pile. He bent over and picked up a new plank, took out a few nails, and pounded them in with a few solid whacks each. The minutes ticked away; half an hour had gone by before he knew it. The weather was getting hot; it was much warmer than when he started out in the morning. He could feel the sweat dripping down his back. Cole seized the sides of his T-shirt and pulled it over his head. He wiped the sweat from his face with the shirt, then tossed it to the side.

Cole heard a slight squeak coming from the screen door as it opened. He turned his head in the direction of the sound. Lucy was standing in the entryway, with two cold drinks in her hands. She stepped slowly forward and stopped a few feet from him.

"Here you go. You must be hot. The sun is beating down since I went inside," she said, extending one of the iced coffees to him. He grasped it and took a long drink, swallowing several times.

"Mmm! That's refreshing! I'm almost done. Only one more board to put in, and that's it," he said. Getting up from his knees, Cole placed his drink on the top of the railing before he went to pick up the last board. He carried it to the platform and laid it in place, then pounded in the last few nails. When he finished, he looked up at Lucy. She was leaning against the wall, just watching him. Cole unhooked his tool belt and dropped it, then went to rest beside her.

"Not bad," he said casually, as he inspected his work. "It just needs to be painted, and you will be all set," he told her, folding his arms across his chest.

"Not bad! It's perfect. I would have never been able to fix it. Thanks a lot," Lucy replied. She glanced at him, then smiled. Her green eyes danced in the sunlight as Cole pointed to the lake.

"I think I'm going for a dip in the lake," he said. He took a step toward the stairs, stopped and stretched out his hand to her. "Coming?" he asked and watched as she wrinkled her nose and bit her lower lip, unsure.

"But I don't have my bathing suit on! Oh, hell... Let's do it," she answered, and placed her hand in his. He grasped it and started to run down to the dock. He could hear her giggle, "Ready?" Cole shouted as they approached the end of the small pier. They jumped into the chilly water together, while holding hands. He lost her hand as she hit the water. He came up to the surface just as she was popping up herself. They were both laughing. He swam next to her, just inches away. Cole reached over underwater and pulled Lucy against his body, and they treaded water together. She didn't resist his embrace, and placed her hands on his shoulders. The cool water could not stop the feeling he had in his groin. She looked so beautiful with strands of auburn hair over her wet face. His lips were inches from hers. Cole looked into Lucy's eyes, and just couldn't help himself. He leaned forward and gently kissed her.

**

Thirty yards away, behind a large oak tree, Rodney Jones' eyes were glued to the woman on the porch. He was strolling down one of the trails with a stick in his hand, passing the time and checking his rabbit traps behind Lucy's bungalow. He spotted her in the driveway as she came out of her SUV. He slowly advanced closer to the house, making sure to stay hidden in the tall grass at the edge of her property. He crouched down low while biting his dirty fingernails.

He watched as she opened the front door; a few minutes later, she came back out. She went back to her car and started carrying boxes, plus a few suitcases, into the home. She seemed to be moving in. He was mesmerized by the way she moved, her red hair flowing in the wind. She was gorgeous. Rodney sat down on the moist ground, hidden by the bushes behind her cottage; he observed her for over an hour from afar. He wondered who she was. How long was she going to stay? His eyes stayed on her.

He wanted to meet her, but not today. She was busy. Rodney took his cell-phone out of his pocket. He aimed it at her and pushed the camera button. He snapped a couple of pictures of the redhead, smiling. He stayed until the sun went down, sitting on the muddy leaves, not moving. She hopped in her truck around suppertime and did not return. He waited for a while, but he got cold and hungry; he was too uncomfortable to stay any longer, so he walked back to his place with her on his mind.

Rodney was in his early thirties. He was a short man, only five feet six inches, with bad posture. His light blond hair was straggly and thinning on the top. His features were homely. He'd always had pimples on his cheeks since he was a teenager. He also wore thick glasses, being born cross-eyed. Rodney's front teeth were decayed; he had not ever taken care of them.

His impoverished grandparents raised him as best as they could afford, when his mother abandoned him at the age of five. His mother had taken off with her drugged-up boyfriend, never to be seen again. Both Rodney's grand-parents had died within the last ten years of old age. He was alone. He'd left high school at the age of sixteen to care for them. He worked in town as one of the helpers for a local mechanic, at Ted's Garage in Houlton. He cleaned the garage after hours, pumped gas, and helped when he could. It didn't pay much, but he got by with what his boss paid him. It was the only job he'd ever held in his life.

He lived in his grandparent's rundown farmhouse, about a mile and a half from this fascinating woman. The poor economy and lack of money stopped him from repairing it to its original form, so it became deplorable. It didn't bother Rodney though, living as he did. He never entertained or had visitors, so no one saw the inside. Not even a handful of people had come to visit in years, and he liked it that way. He liked being a loner. A recluse—that's what some people called him. Rodney didn't listen to them. Living this way, no one told him what to do, like clean the house or bathe or do repairs to his house. He did his own thing. He rarely spoke to anyone, but his boss, always keeping his head bowed low, and his eyes averted from anyone else's sight. The only man he had to obey and talk to was old man Ted, his employer, because he didn't want to lose his job. He barely had expenses, so most of his pay was untouched. Rodney saved it; he didn't need much.

Rodney sat at the kitchen table that evening eating beans from a can. He looked up at the dirty dishes and empty take-out boxes with leftover, rotten food scattered around the counter. He looked at the clock on the wall. It was almost ten o'clock. *I have to pick up this mess one day*, he thought. He put his fork down next to the can. He contemplated returning to the woman's house to see if she was back. He took out his phone and clicked on photos he had taken earlier in the day. A picture of Lucy appeared on his phone. He touched the screen with his finger and licked his lips. Rodney stood up and put on his jacket. He decided to go see if she was home yet; he really wanted to see her again. He ran out the back door, not even bothering to lock it.

He loved walking in the woods at night; he wasn't afraid. The moon and the stars eliminated his path. He felt like a cougar roaming the forest for its prey. Rodney smirked at the thought. He placed his hands in his pockets and continued until he arrived at the edge of her property. He bent down on one knee in the tree line and observed the house. The lights were on the inside, and she was in the back. He could see her as she walked by the living room window. *I wonder what her name is, and how long she's staying,* he thought.

Rodney waited patiently, his eyes glued on the window, hoping to see her move past it once more—but she didn't. He wanted to see her one more time before he returned home. He slowly rose up halfway, keeping low to the ground as he advanced toward the light of the house. He had his back against the rear wall of the bungalow within minutes. He breathed through his nose heavily, trying to stay quiet and control his breathing. He had never done something like spy on a woman before, and he felt nervous—but also sexually excited.

He could hear the crickets chirping and the wind rustling through the leaves. His hands were sweaty. He wiped them on his pants. His head was near a small window, and he could hear music coming from inside. Rodney turned toward it and decided to peek in to see if he could get a glimpse of her. As he turned, his foot caught one of the wheels on the garbage can, and the container tipped to one side. He grabbed at it to catch it and stop it from falling, but he missed. It made a loud noise as it hit the ground. He froze, not moving for a minute. Rodney's heart pounded hard against his chest; afraid of being caught, he closed his eyes tightly. His ears strained to catch any sounds the woman might make. Nothing! He slowly moved away from the house, being careful of where he placed his every step. When he arrived at the corner of the bungalow, he ran the last few yards back to the cover of the dense shrubbery growing in the tree line. He dove to the ground behind the bushes.

That was close! I'll have to be more careful next time, he thought, as he tried to catch his breath and relax. Rodney took one last look at the house before he returned home. She hadn't come out, so she couldn't have heard him. He would come back later. He turned around and headed back the way he had come, back to the farmhouse.

Chapter 3

It was the middle of July. The heat of the summer was in full bloom. It had been two weeks since she drove up the lane to her new place of residence. Lucy sat on her veranda admiring the glare of the sun upon the lake while drinking her ice tea. She raised her feet up on the railing of the porch to relax. She closed her eyes as she felt the warm breeze from the lake against her face. The covered porch was the perfect place for her to relax, since she wasn't one to go in the direct sun; her skin would burn and she would end up being all pink, at least. Lucy mused about her new boyfriend, Cole.

She and Cole had talked a lot about their pasts, and one day last week he'd asked her why she never married. She thought about telling him she hadn't found the right man, but she didn't want to start this relationship by lying to him. Sitting on the couch next to him, her eyes filled with tears and she turned her head to the side while playing with his chest., Bothered by the thought of her husband. Cole placed his hand under her chin and moved her face back toward him. He said, "It's okay. You don't have to tell me now. Just whenever you are ready, I'll be here." He smiled at her. A tear had slipped down her cheek. He gently took his finger and wiped it away without a word.

Lucy finally confided in him later that day and told him the circumstances surrounding her husband's death. He was sympathetic as he listened. Cole held her close in his arms as she spoke. He didn't question her until she was finished. He gave her soft kisses without pressuring her to go any further. He whispered in her ear, "It's all in the past. I'm here for you now."

She forgot all the misfortunes of her past when she was near him; Lucy's heart was mending slowly. She hadn't known Cole long, but she liked everything about him. He was handsome, kind, smart, and she loved the way he touched her: so tenderly without expecting more. He was patient! On many occasions she had felt him against her body, wanting, yearning for her. He pulled away every time, waiting for her to make the next move. She didn't have to courage, even though she had the desire.

She brought her drink to her mouth to savor the cool wetness while waiting for Cole. She looked at her watch; it was seven o'clock. Cole should arrive soon for supper. She took the few footsteps to the door and entered the house. He should be off his shift soon. Lucy opened the icebox to gather two steaks and the vegetables for the salad. She placed it all on the counter, then grabbed a knife and started chopping the lettuce on the cutting board. She then cut up tomatoes and cucumbers, dropping them all in a wooden bowl. Lucy pushed the bowl to the side and took the T-bone steaks out of the wrapper next, placing them on a plate to season them with salt and pepper.

She was distracted from her work when she heard a motorcycle coming up her driveway. Lucy glanced out the window and then walked to the entrance to greet her man. It was Cole. She waved to him, her heart swelling at the sight of him. Her desire for him mounted. He parked the bike, dismounted, and hooked his helmet on the handlebar. He was wearing a pair of tight black jeans and a black Harley Davidson T-shirt. He took the steps two at a time. She opened the screen door and within seconds, his arms were wrapped around her. He lifted her from the ground. He kissed her on the lips, then said, "You smell good enough to eat," She smiled at him as she slapped his shoulder lightly. Lucy could feel the heat rise to her face.

"I have two T-bone steaks waiting to be barbecued, and salad," she answered him as they entered the cottage.

"I'll settle for that...for now," he grinned at her, kissed her neck then let her go. She watched as he walked to the kitchen counter and grabbed the plate with the steaks.

"I didn't put the grill on yet; can you manage? I'm going to set us up in the gazebo. What do you think?" she asked as she filled a large basket with a tablecloth, plates, utensils, and a bottle of Merlot.

"That sounds romantic!" Cole replied.

Lucy trekked to the gazebo and prepared a cozy spot for them. She lit a few candles and placed open-topped glass spheres on top of them to keep them from being blown out by the evening breeze. She had brought a few pillows from the house earlier; she set them on the floor with the rest of the things. Lucy took a step back and admired her spot. "Perfect!"

She went to join Cole, who already had the meat on the barbecue. The steaks sizzled on the grill. She could smell the aroma of the spices on the steaks. Lucy wrapped her arms around Cole's waist from behind, and kissed him on the back of the neck.

"Mmm! You shouldn't do that when I'm cooking. I might forget about the food," he said as he rotated his body to face her. He cupped her face in the palms of his hands, and his lips came bearing down on hers. His tongue explored her mouth, causing a sexual feeling to travel quickly through her, making her legs weak. Lucy had to pull away to catch her breath.

"I think your steaks are burning," she glanced at him just in time to see the flames swallow up the meat.

"Oh, shit!" he said, and hurriedly moved them to the right of the grill with the tongs. She laughed loudly, and he soon joined in her hysterics.

"It's all your fault," Cole teased her, placing the meat into a dish. She moved toward the kitchen, intending to grab the salad in one hand and the glasses for the wine in the other.

"I'll meet you in the gazebo," Lucy shouted his way, still snickering. She hurried, and within two minutes she was standing at the entrance of the hexagonal gazebo.

"Come sit beside me and eat the masterpiece of a steak I made," Cole said. He tapped the cushion on his right side. Lucy scurried to sit beside him. He gave her a plate with her steak, and she served him a salad. He poured two glasses of wine, then passed one to her. Cole lifted his glass for a toast. "To the two of us," he said, then leaned forward and kissed her lips lightly. They talked while they ate and in an hour finished the bottle of wine. She laughed at all his jokes, and when his arm brought her close to his body and pushed her on her back, she didn't resist. Her arms went around his neck, and when he looked into her eyes she nodded at him. Cole kissed her passionately and when his wet mouth nibbled on her ear, she lifted her hips to meet him. She could feel his hand under her shirt on her bare stomach, inching upward toward her breasts. Lucy decided it was time to move on and let love come back in her life. She needed him, she wanted him, and most of all she trusted him.

Forty-five minutes later, Cole lay naked on his back, breathing hard on the floor of the gazebo, staring at the ceiling. Lucy playfully kissed his neck as she lay next to him on her belly, her red hair spread across his abdomen, his arm wrapped around her waist. He lifted his head and reached for the blanket that was on the chair next to them, draping it over their bodies.

"That was worth waiting for," Cole said in a low voice. He rubbed her back with his fingers and kissed the top of her head.

"I sure hope it will continue, and we can do it over, and over..." she replied, giggling and hiding her face in his chest. He leaned up and kissed her on the nose.

***

Over the last two weeks, he'd grown to love her funny side and most of all how beautiful she was inside and out. Cole wanted to spend as much time as he could with her. Lucy had a hold on him that he couldn't deny, from the first time he laid eyes on her. He didn't want to move as she snuggled against his body. He relished every time she touched him.

"Would you like to spend the night with me?' he heard her say. A smile came across his face as she looked up at him for his response.

"I would love to; and every other night, if you let me," he told her as he pushed a strand of her auburn hair from her face. She stroked his chest.

"What are the chances I could run to the house without being seen?" Lucy asked, lifting herself on her elbows.

"There a high probability I will have to arrest you for indecent exposure. I will definitely watch and try to catch you in the act," he sniggered, and then slapped her on the butt.

"Okay...catch me if you can," she said as she slowly moved away from him. He felt a chill where she had been laying on top of him. He sat up and extended his arms to grab her, but she was too quick. Cole let his fingers slip away from his grip as Lucy wiggled her way out the door. He watched her as she sprinted to the back door of the house. He bent down, picked up his jeans, and dashed after her.

The next morning Cole woke up at dawn, as he did every day for work. He turned his head to his left; Lucy slept soundly by his side,; her arm draped across his chest. He quietly slipped out of bed without waking her up. He stood by the bed admiring her while he put his clothes on. Her messed-up hair shrouded the pillow and her half-naked body made him want to jump back in bed. He leaned over her to gently pull the comforter over her shoulders. Lucy stirred without waking up. He tip-toed out of the room and walked to the kitchen. He opened the drawers until he found pen and paper. He wrote her a note, then placed it by her coffee pot where he knew she would find it.

Cole had to return home to shower and get into his uniform before he went to work.

He mounted his bike, put his helmet on, and drove slowly away. All the way home, his thoughts were on Lucy. He liked everything about this woman, especially her laughter and how caring and attentive she was to his needs. He could spend the rest of his life with her. Cole had never felt this strongly about any woman. He loved her quirky ways and when she blushed or giggled at anything. He wanted to devote most of his time to this relationship and see where it would lead. Soon Cole turned into his driveway and parked his bike. He ran inside and headed directly to his bathroom to shower. Cole turned the water on and threw his clothes to the side in a rush. Within minutes, he was washed, dressed in his state trooper uniform, and ready to go to work.

***

Rodney missed the woman with the red hair. He was so busy with work he hadn't been able to go see her for a few days. Broom in hand, he was in one of the bays in the garage sweeping the floor toward the outside. She was constantly on his mind; he smirked just at the thought of seeing her hair flow in the wind as it had the last time he had seen her. That was almost a week ago. Yes, he wanted to go see her, either tonight or early in the morning before work. He would find the time to go see her.

It was the end of the month, and motorists needed vehicle inspection stickers for their cars. He also pumped the gas in the full-service department, so he couldn't leave early to go check on her. He only saw her through the window of her house, most days. Rodney was afraid to get too close, worried he would be discovered—but she was always in his heart. He had never felt this way for a woman before. He had to find a way to make her his.

He heard the bell that alerted him someone was at full service for gasoline. He leaned his broom against the wall and took a step toward the gas pumps. A Range Rover was parked in front of the unleaded pump. Rodney froze on the spot. He couldn't move; he held his breath. Rodney couldn't believe his eyes. It was *her*.

"Rodney, you have a customer," Ted shouted, wiping his hands on a dirty old rag and pointing. Rodney raised his hand and nodded at Ted. He pulled his oily cap down lower on his head before approaching the Range Rover to stand next to her door. He watched expressionless as her window came down. The woman smiled his way and said, "Fill it up please, with supreme." Her voice was music to his ears. He detected a flowery scent coming from her. Without a word he nodded his head and walked around to the back of the truck, opened the cap, then grabbed the nozzle from the pump. He pressed the button and started the flow of the gas, but never took his eyes off of her. He stared through the back window, stunned. *She is more beautiful up close*, he thought. *I wonder what her name is?*

The spout clicked that the tank was full. He felt a wave of disappointment that she was going to leave now. He replaced the nozzle and walked near the passenger window. He picked up the handle of the squeegee to clean her windshield. He stepped to the side and washed the window, and continued to watch her from the corner of his eye. She smiled at him. Rodney looked away. He should have smiled back, but his teeth were yellow—and a few of them rotten. He was embarrassed. No one ever took the time to acknowledge him in any nice way. Finally, he took two strides and was standing next to the driver's door.

"Forty-five dollars, please," he managed to say. Rodney's mouth was dry from the excitement of talking to her. He licked his lips several times. She handed him her credit card, which he took inside the garage to swipe it in the credit card machine. The name on the card was Lucy Marvin. He kept repeating her name in his head, over and over—*Lucy, Lucy Marvin.*

Rodney ripped the receipt off the machine and took it to her. As he gave it to her, his fingers brushed against hers.

"Thank you for washing my windshield. Have a nice day," she told him. She started the engine and drove off.

"Thank *you*, Lucy Marvin," he whispered as he watched the SUV depart. Rodney stood by the pumps until he couldn't see her; she disappeared down the street too soon. *Lucy told me to have a nice day!* She liked him, and she wasn't a stuck up bitch like most of the females he encountered at the station. He wanted to do something for her, for being so pleasant. Most people in town didn't even acknowledge him—and if they did, they usually made fun of him. He didn't like it. They considered him a slacker, a ne'er-do-well. Ted felt sorry for him, so he gave him a side job when he was a teenager. Rodney pushed his straggly blond hair behind his ear, with his hand then he returned to the bay to finish his work.

***

After work that evening, Rodney set his alarm clock for five o'clock in the morning, two hours earlier than he normally got up. It rang on time. He reached over and turned it off, sat up immediately, and grabbed the soiled blue employee coveralls that rested beside his bed on the floor. He placed his feet into the legs and zipped it up, then hurriedly laced his boots. Within minutes of waking, he walked out of his home. The sun hadn't even come up yet. Rodney rushed to the large field behind his house, where lots of wildflowers grew. He bent down and gathered daisies, coneflowers, purple loosestrifes, and many others.

Rodney examined his bouquet as he held it. in his hand. He shoved his other hand in his pocket and pulled out a pink ribbon he had brought from home, tying a bow around the stems. He took a shortcut through the woods, sprinting over rocks and around dead branches. Rodney quickly arrived at the edge of the forest near Lucy's cottage and scrutinized the property to see if it was safe to go forward. *Since there are no lights on, she must still be asleep.*

He noticed there was a motorcycle parked in the driveway that he hadn't seen before. She had company. He wondered if whoever was driving this bike was a man; it was probably hers. He rubbed his face with his hands and wondered if he should go peek through her window to find out. Rodney crouched down for a moment. With the flowers in one hand, he scampered as fast as he could toward the front of the house, keeping an eye out for any lights coming on. He stopped near the veranda, then slowly tiptoed up the steps until he was on the porch. Rodney's eyes swept the porch, trying to figure out where to leave the flowers. He noticed a rocking chair near the door, so he carefully laid them on the seat. He turned around without making any noise, dashed down the steps, and ran back into the woods, being careful not to wake her or be seen. He stopped at the perimeter of the woods, crouched down, and looked back for about five minutes. His heartbeat racing, he squatted down near the high grass and took one last look through the leaves. *I hope she likes the flowers*, he thought. He got up and continued back down the trail to get back home, then go to work.

Chapter 4

Lucy was awake, but she kept her eyes closed. She lay on her belly, her head turned toward Cole. She moved her hand across the bed to feel for Cole, but all she found was a cold bed sheet. She opened her eyes and raised up on her elbows. She didn't see him. He wasn't there.

"Cole?" she said loudly. She listened, but there was no answer. She rose, slipped on her bathrobe that was on the chair next to her bed. Lucy headed for the kitchen, wishing he were still by her side. She noticed the folded paper near the coffee machine and opened it carefully. She smiled as she read the note.

> Good morning, Beautiful,
> Sorry I had to sneak out, but duty calls.
> I had a fantastic time last night, and I'll be back for more.
> I'll call later tonight for supper,
> Cole

She brought the paper to her chest, holding it over her heart. She pushed the on button on the coffee machine then just stood by the counter watching the coffee drip as she closed her eyes and sighed. Lucy reminisced about the evening they had shared. She had deep feelings for this man, and she was excited about spending more time with him.

"It's time for another love in your life, Lucy," she said out loud, as she grabbed a cup from the cupboard and poured herself a cup of coffee. She walked to the front door porch and opened the main door. Leaning against the doorframe, she looked out toward the lake. The sun was bright, and she could already feel the heat on her face. She'd brought her mug to her mouth to take a sip of her coffee when she saw a bouquet of wildflowers tied with a ribbon, on her rocking chair by the door. She pushed the screen door open and picked up the flowers. She inhaled the fragrance, assuming they were from Cole. *How thoughtful!* She turned around, went to the cabinet to find a vase, and pushed the knob on the radio as she walked by it. Music came flowing through the house. Lucy placed the bouquet on the kitchen island and danced all the way to her bathroom to take a shower. She was happy! Lucy decided she needed to go to town to buy groceries to make Cole a special meal.

An hour later, she pinned up her hair in a messy bun, put on a flowered cotton dress, and didn't bother to put on underwear. It would be a surprise for Cole. She swung the strap of her bag over her shoulder and headed for the door. As she passed by the flowers on the counter, Lucy stopped and plucked two daisies from the vase. She pushed her hair behind her ear, then attached the flowers with a bobby pin. She examined her masterpiece in the mirror on the way out the door. She hopped in her Range Rover and was on her way to the supermarket.

The town of New Limerick didn't have any major supermarkets, so she drove to Houlton, where there was a Hannaford store. She parked, picked up the grocery list on the passenger seat, hopped out and walked toward the entrance. She pulled a cart from the wall and went inside. Lucy strolled from aisle to aisle, depositing items in her cart she needed to make a delicious dish for supper for Cole. She was at the meat counter trying to decide what to get when an eerie feeling came over her. A chill ran down her back, as if someone was observing her. She turned her head to look over her shoulder, but she didn't see anyone near her. She shook off the feeling and finished shopping. She walked to the front and got in line at the checkout counter. She placed some of her groceries on the belt and waited for her turn.

"Nice flowers," she heard someone say. She turned and saw the man that had pumped her gas the previous day at the gas station. He was pointing at the flowers in her hair. She didn't want to be impolite or rude to him, so she touched the daisies in her hair and said, "Yes, they are, thank you," and continued to place the rest of her things on the belt one at a time. The cashier greeted her and scanned her items. She only had two bags, so she decided to carry them in her arms instead of using her cart. Lucy exited the store and was about to cross into the parking lot when she realized someone was talking to her again.

"Let me help you with the bags." She looked to her right, and the guy from the gas station was beside her with his arms extended toward her bags. She felt unsure about him. *Is he following me?* she thought. She didn't want to hurt his feelings, and maybe he was only friendly. She knew people from this small town often helped each other, so she nodded at him and gave him a small smile.

"Thank you," she said and handed the two heavy bags to him. He took them and walked beside her with his head lowered.

"You're the gas attendant, aren't you?" she asked. He just nodded and continued walking beside her.

"What's your name?" she questioned him just to make conversation. Lucy didn't want him to feel uncomfortable, since he was good enough to carry her bags.

"Rodney Jones, miss," was all he uttered, still not looking her way.

"Nice to make your acquaintance Rodney, and thanks again," she told him. She took her keys from her pocketbook and opened the trunk for him to put the groceries inside. She watched as he placed them inside carefully, and he stood back while the door shut and locked.

"Thank you," she said and took a few strides to the driver's door, opened it and sat inside. She observed him in the rearview mirror. He stood to the side of her truck rubbing his hands together. He turned in a moment, and almost seemed to be skipping, returning to his place of employment, which was located beside the supermarket. Lucy inhaled deeply, then let it out slowly. She was glad he was gone. She felt a little uneasy around him, but she concluded it was because of his appearance. *He was only being courteous. He didn't mean you any harm,* she thought to herself. Feeling foolish, she pushed aside the thoughts and pushed the button to start her Range Rover. She was soon headed to her bungalow to prepare her love a great meal.

***

When Rodney arrived at work, he was feeling content with his early-morning errand, leaving the flowers for her on the porch. He would see her again. He was cleaning the pumps outside when he saw her SUV pass by. He stopped polishing immediately, and dropped his cloth to spy on her. He rushed to the edge of the lot just in time to see her entering the store. Rodney took his cap off and raked his fingers through his soiled hair. He looked toward the bays of the garage and yelled to his boss, "I'm going to get some lunch at the supermarket." He didn't wait for Ted to answer. He marched as fast as he could to the market. He searched the aisles until he finally saw her. He hid behind one of the displays and watched her every move, following her from aisle to aisle. *She's wearing the daisies I gave her in her hair,* he thought, amazed. He pulled back against the wall as his heart swelled with love for his woman. No one had ever made such a show of affection for him. She *must* like him. He needed to talk to her again, to show her he cared for her—but how was he going to do that? He had discreetly trailed her as she shopped down the aisles until she went to the checkout counter. It took all Rodney's courage to talk to her, as beads of sweat formed down his back.

She didn't send him away or ignore him, as most women did. She had even asked him his name after he carried her bags to her truck. She was the most beautiful woman in the world, to him. He would do anything for her. She was his, and she belonged to him from now on. He could feel an erection grow as he thought about her. He would go to her house this evening to see her. He watched her pull out of the parking lot. Rodney hurried back to work with lots of hope in his heart.

***

Rodney's day passed slowly. He counted every minute on the clock as he worked. He avoided his boss all afternoon, hoping he could sneak out early. Finally, five o'clock came. He rushed out without speaking to anyone. He didn't want Ted to ask him to stay a little longer; Rodney slipped out when Ted told him he was going to the bathroom. He grabbed his bicycle and pedaled as fast as he could in the direction of his house. Sweat was dripping down his face by the time he entered the kitchen. He walked to the sink, picked up a tumbler, and gulped down a glass of water. On the way over to the farmhouse, he'd remembered his grandmother had binoculars somewhere in the house. She used to bird watch off her veranda. If he could find them, he could get a better view of Lucy when he observed her from the tall weeds of the forest.

Rodney ran to his grandmother's bedroom. Opening all of the dresser drawers and finding nothing, he turned his search to the closet. He swung the door open wide and reached up for the stack of boxes. Rodney laid them on top of his grandmother's purple bedspread, combing through every container to no avail. His temper mounted when he still couldn't find the binoculars. With a swift shove of his hand, he pushed the empty boxes off the bed. They tumbled down on the floor, papers and photos spreading everywhere. He balled his fists and punched the mattress, furious at not finding the binoculars.

"Calm down, and think! Where would she have put them?" he said out loud, as he sat on her bed biting his already raw fingernails. His eyes wandered around the room. *Yes—her side table.* Rodney opened the drawer and smiled as he snatched them, then walked out of the room. He put the strap around his neck, and grabbed his backpack from the back of the chair. Rodney added a bottle of water and two granola bars to the bag, and was almost ready to head out the door. He picked up one more item, the most important thing: a large pair of scissors that were on the counter top. He stuffed everything in the backpack and swung it over his shoulder.

Rodney rushed out the back door. He crossed his yard and hurried up the trail, stopping at one point to change direction. He took the course that would lead him to Lucy's bungalow, and twenty minutes later, he saw his destination in front of him. He slowed his pace, being careful not to fall or make any noise. He crouched down until he arrived in front of the bushes, his excitement mounting at the prospect of seeing her again.

He shoved his hand into the pocket of his bag and took out the instrument that would give him a clear view: the scissors. Rodney snipped the tiny branches of the bush one at a time, until a viewing hole was created. Now his view would not be obstructed, yet he couldn't be seen. He would be able to observe Lucy's every movement from where he was now sitting. Rodney looked around his surroundings for a large rock or log to sit on. He saw a rock that looked to be the right size, and pulled on it with all his might. It resisted for a moment but soon came loose, and he moved it to the exact spot where he'd made the window in the bushes. Perching on top of the rock, he thought, *Perfect!* He grasped his binoculars and focused his sight on her.

There she was, in the kitchen. She was at the island cutting something. She looked beautiful in her sundress with her hair down. Bare shoulders, her firm breasts just showing a little cleavage: just enough to entice. She sang and danced around the room, her hips swaying from side to side. He could hear faint music coming from the open window. He felt saliva oozing down the side of his chin. He licked his upper lip, wondering how she would taste. He was feeling funny again; the feeling from that afternoon at the store, a sensation he never had before, overwhelmed his groin. Rodney felt a hot shiver pass through him as he pulled his eyes away for a moment.

He set his sight rest on her again. She was on the phone talking to someone; she laughed and passed her hand through her auburn hair. Suddenly, her expression changed. She seemed sad or disappointed. Lucy bowed her head, then hung up the phone. *Who was on the line that altered her mood?* He watched as she reached over and shut off the radio. She gathered the food and placed it in containers, then put them in the refrigerator. Maybe she was expecting company and something happened. She drank the rest of her wine and refilled her glass.

Rodney followed her movements as she moved to another room with a wine glass in her hand. It was partially obstructed by a tree near the window. He waited for her to reappear. She soon did, with a shawl around her shoulders. She waltzed through the kitchen and opened the back door. She sat down on the rocking chair on the porch facing the lake, the outdoor light illuminating her. Lucy didn't budge for a whole hour just staring out at the water.

Rodney moved to the left to get a better view of her. His foot caught in a twisted root; he stumbled forward and fell down. He didn't stir for a second. He just listened for movement. Nothing! He crawled on his hands and knees over to the next bush. He couldn't see her any better because the tall grass was too high. He took his hand and slowly pushed the grass to one side, and saw her get up and enter the house again. She shut the door behind her, then went to the living room and closed the shades. He saw the light in her bedroom go on, but he couldn't see her; the curtains were closed.

Should he call it a night and go home, or wait to see if she would come back out where he could see her? Rodney drummed his fingers on his leg, waiting. He took a granola bar out of his bag and ate it. He hadn't had supper, and he was hungry.

Another half hour passed. The stars were out, and the moon was shining over the water. *She probably went to bed.* He felt disappointed she had gone inside. Rodney scratched his head, then rubbed his chin. *I might as well go home,* he decided. He rose, taking one last peek at the bungalow, and walked away. He dragged his feet down the trail, kicking the leaves as he strolled back to his house, feeling upset and let down. *I'll bring her more flowers tomorrow, since she liked them so much. It will make her happy,* he thought. *I don't like to see her sad.*

Chapter 5

Lucy hadn't slept very well. She'd tossed and turned most of the night. She kept the light in the bathroom on all night, and her eyes glued to the entrance of her bedroom until she fell asleep. She thought she had seen the figure of a man hiding behind the bushes near her house the previous night, while she was sitting on the porch drinking her wine. She saw a movement in the bushes, and kept telling herself it was probably an animal—but it frightened her enough that she walked inside, locked the doors, and kept her cellphone in hand. If she heard any more noise outside or even detected a shadow near her windows or doors, she was going to call Cole right away.

Cole had called early in the evening from his squad car. He wouldn't be able to make it to dinner because he had to work a double shift. One of his colleagues was injured pursuing a thief on foot earlier in the day, and Cole had to help with the investigation at the scene. He probably wouldn't be back until really late, so he told her he would come by tomorrow afternoon.

The sun came through the blinds of her bedroom like lasers, making her squint as she turned over on her side. She raised her hand to shelter her eyes, as liked to lie in bed in the early morning hours. She soon decided just to get up, so she slipped on her robe and walked to the kitchen. Lucy was still tired from the restless night. She rubbed the back of her neck as she watched the coffee slowly drip into the pot. Finally, she poured a cup, added cream, and headed toward the front door. She unlocked the door and glanced at the lake while sipping her drink. She pushed the screen door open slowly and took the few steps toward her rocking chair.

Lucy stopped as a chill ran down her back when she thought of her fear from last night. She gasped. Her hand went weak; her coffee cup slipped from her grip and shattered on the porch. There, on the seat of the rocking chair, was another bouquet of wildflowers tied with a pink ribbon. She looked from side to side, scanning the area, trying to see who could have left them. She hoped they were from Cole, but realized he couldn't have brought them. He was working all night. Lucy was positive the wildflowers were not there last night, because she was sitting where they lay. Her hands and knees started to shake when it registered that someone had been on her porch during the night and left her flowers. *That's really frightening–and creepy!* she thought.

This time, she didn't touch them. Lucy stepped backward from them as if they were poisoned, and reentered the house as quickly as possible. She locked the door immediately and marched directly to her bedroom. She grabbed a pair of jeans and a light sweater from the closet and dressed quickly. *Who is leaving these flowers?* She didn't know many people in town. Her heart started beating faster as she peeked out the window. Everything looked undisturbed and normal. But what about the shadow she'd noticed the previous night? *Was that my imagination, or was there someone watching me by the woods? You are being paranoid, Lucy; this is a small friendly town. You aren't in the city anymore. No one does this kind of stuff here.*

She looked at the clock in the hallway; it was only eight o'clock. She knew Cole worked the overnight shift, so he was probably sleeping. She would wait a few hours. Lucy went to sit on the couch where she could see both doors, and tried to calm her nerves down. She picked up a magazine from the side table and started to leaf through it.

She sat unmoving, trying futilely to concentrate on reading an article. Her ears twitched at every sound, her eyes darting everywhere; after a half hour, she gave up. She threw the magazine on top of the cushion. *Stop it right now! This is ridiculous!* Lucy got up, brushed her stupid ideas away, and went to the kitchen to make toast for breakfast. She realized she wasn't hungry yet when she picked up the bread, so she decided to go out for breakfast in town instead. It would get her out of the house until Cole was up. She had to stop worrying over this idiotic thought that she was in danger.

Lucy brushed her hair and put on lipstick. She determinedly marched to the door, unlocked it, and stepped outside. Her eyes were drawn to the untouched flowers on the chair as she passed it, but she quickened her pace. She marched down the stairs to her SUV, turned on the engine, and departed down the dirt road to town.

Lucy drove into town, parked on Main Street, then sauntered down the street stopping to window shop. A boutique caught her eyes across the street. It was an arts and crafts store. *I should be able to pass some time in there*, she thought. Browsing in the shop, she found a few items she wanted, like a hanging angel and a serving dish with a sailboat on a lake. She paid for them, then the sales-person wrapped and placed them in a shopping bag.

Lucy felt better, forgetting about the flowers. She left the store and drove down the road to the Ma and Pop restaurant where she had met Cole to have a hearty breakfast. She was famished by the time she arrived.

"Good morning, Harry!" Lucy said. She passed by him on her way to the booth she chose to sit in, dropping her bag at her feet under the table. He was behind the counter, serving coffee to a customer on one of the stools.

"Morning Lucy, I'll be right over. Have a seat," he answered. She noticed the person he was serving. *It's the guy from the gas station, what's his name... Rodney*, she thought. He was sitting at the counter eating pancakes. He shyly looked at her from underneath his cap. *Pancakes. That sounds pretty good right now*, she thought. She looked up in Harry's direction, and he pointed to the coffee pot. She nodded. He came forward, served it and handed her a menu.

"Do you know what you would like?" he asked casually, then stood by the table waiting.

"I'll just have an order of blueberry pancakes," she told him. That seemed appetizing with golden syrup.

"And Harry, can you add an order of bacon?" she asked, as she gave him back the menu. She added cream to her coffee, stirred it slowly with her spoon, then took a sip. Lucy looked around at the other patrons while waiting for her order. The man from the garage who was sitting at the counter kept glancing at her, then he smiled her way. She didn't want to be impolite, so she returned it, then she turned her head to look outside the window.

Within minutes, Harry was back with pancakes, bacon and syrup. He placed the dishes in front of her. Lucy thanked him and immediately picked up her fork to dig into them. She was almost finished with her meal when she noticed someone was standing next to her. She looked up to see Rodney. He had his head bowed and his cap in his hands. He seemed nervous, and she noticed he was squeezing his hat in his hands tightly. She looked up at him and said, "Hi, Rodney, how are you today?" Lucy smiled, trying not to make him feel uncomfortable.

He just stood still for a moment, then answered, "Fine, thank you." A silent moment came between them. She figured he was just shy.

"Did you enjoy your pancakes?" She asked him pleasantly. He just nodded at her. She saw him shift his weight from one foot to another.

"No flowers today?" he asked. He pointed to the top of her hair, where she had pinned two daisies the previous day. Lucy swallowed hard as she remembered the flowers, and lost her appetite. She put her fork on the plate.

"No, not today," was all she said. She wiped her mouth with her napkin, then pushed her plate away from her. Lucy didn't want to be rude, but he was just standing next to her, and there was a really bad, sweaty smell coming from his oily overalls. She reached over and took out her wallet to pay the check, but he wasn't saying or doing anything. He just stood there. She picked up her bill and looked up at him.

"I'm sorry, Rodney, but I have to get going. You have a nice day," Lucy said. She was trying to slide out of the booth, but he was still blocking her way.

"Oh! I have to get back to work too," he replied, and moved to the side so she could stand. Lucy glanced at him and saw his face had turned red, probably from embarrassment at being in her way. She felt bad so she smiled and told him, "I have to go so I'll see you later, Rodney."

He bashfully smiled as he put his cap on his head. "Yeah! Okay, 'bye," he replied as she walked past him. Lucy headed toward the counter, where Harry was standing. She gave him her check and took a twenty out of her wallet. The time on the clock behind the counter read noon. She walked back to her vehicle and dialed Cole's number. Lucy waited patiently while it rang for the third time. *Maybe he's still sleeping*, she thought. She briefly looked in her rear view mirror. She saw Rodney getting on his bicycle and riding away down the road.

"Hi, how are you? I was just going to call you. Are you home?" Cole said in his husky, drowsy voice. She held the phone tighter to her ear as a good feeling passed through her, happy to hear his voice.

"Hi. You seem sleepy; did I wake you?" she asked, turning the key to start the engine. The Bluetooth in her SUV took over, so she dropped her phone in the cup holder. Both hands on the wheel, she backed out of the parking lot.

"No, I just came out of the shower. Sorry about dinner last night, it couldn't be helped. What are you up to today?" he inquired.

"I'm on my way home. I just had breakfast in town at Ma and Pop. Could you come by this afternoon? I need to talk to you about something, and I really don't want to get into it over the phone," she told him, hoping he would meet her.

"Sure. Are you okay? You have me concerned now. How about I meet you in about half an hour?" he asked.

She sighed with relief as she drove back to her bungalow. "Perfect! I will see you then. Miss you, 'bye," she told him. Lucy hung up the phone, grateful he could meet her right away.

Twenty minutes later, she was back at home. She brought in her purchases and put them away. Anxious to see Cole, Lucy kept peeking out the front window while pacing from the living room to the kitchen. Finally, she heard his motorcycle. She swung the door open and stepped on the porch. She waved to him as he approached the house, and watched as he disembarked and placed his helmet on the handlebar. Cole was beside her on the porch in three strides. He reached out and pulled her close to his body. He kissed her on the mouth with a small moan.

"Hi, I missed you," he told her, staring into her eyes.

Lucy smiled. "Missed you too," she answered him. She took his hand in hers and led him inside.

"So tell me, what did you want to talk to me about?" he asked her immediately. He sat down on one of the stools at the counter and took off his sunglasses, then looked at her for an answer. She stood beside him, shifting from foot to foot, unsure if it was worth talking about now that he was here. It was just strange...

"Well, it might be nothing. Yesterday morning, after you left I went to have my coffee on the back veranda. There was a bouquet of flowers on the rocker. At first, I thought they were from you." Lucy stopped talking to take a deep breath, trying to keep her voice steady. She looked toward the back door. Cole brushed his hand down her arm, then squeezed it to show her she could continue when she was ready.

"No, I didn't send them. Do you have a secret admirer I don't know about?" He said it in a playful tone, but his features became serious when she shook her head and tears stung her eyes. He didn't smile when he saw she was about to cry.

"What else?" he asked.

Lucy sat down on the stool beside Cole. He placed his hands on her knee and waited for her response. "I received another bouquet this morning. They were delivered during the night, because they weren't there when I went to bed last night. I'm scared," she said in a low voice.

"Show me. Did you touch them?" he asked as he stood. She led the way toward the back door; Cole pushed the door open, and saw them immediately. He picked up the bouquet and looked at it, scowling.

"Wildflowers? There's no card. Was there one on the first bunch?"

Lucy just shook her head. Cole placed the flowers back on the chair.

"And there's more," she uttered. He whipped his head around to look at her and waited for her to speak, his eyes on hers. "I thought I saw something move over there by the woods last night, but I didn't go check. I figured it was an animal. It startled me, so I went inside," she continued, pointing toward the high grass and bushes at the edge of the woods.

"Stay here. I'll check," Cole said. He walked toward the edge of the bushes and pushed the high grass apart, then went around the shrubbery. He bent down and seemed to be picking something up.

"What are you doing? Did you find something?" Lucy yelled.

He yelled back right away. "One minute; stay there, I'll be right back."

Lucy watched as he took a few more steps inward, then turned around and came back to stand next to her.

"Listen, I'm not sure. I found these wrappers on the ground. It was probably an animal that smelled it and thought it was food. That's what frightened you, silly," he said, showing her the granola bar wrappers.

"Come on, let's go do something today. How about we go for a ride on my bike? I don't have to be back on the night shift at eight o'clock today. We can pick up some food and relax at my place for the afternoon. Maybe you can stay with me for a few days and..." he offered as he wrapped his arms around her waist and repeatedly kissed her neck. She could feel his whiskers as they skimmed her neck once again, and a warm shiver passed down her back.

"And bring your bathing suit. We can swim, and..." he whispered against her skin.

"That sounds like a plan. Let me pack a few things in a backpack and I'll be right back, okay?" she answered, and gently pushed him away. She hurried to the bedroom and threw a bikini, shorts, and a white sundress in a bag. Lucy was overjoyed she was going to spend a few days with Cole at his house.

Chapter 6

Cole stood on the porch, looking out toward the trees. He had a bad feeling about what was going on with these flowers. Someone had been there; someone was watching her. He leaned against the post of the porch, crossed his arms over his chest and mused about the wrappers. He was sure it wasn't any animal, because he had found a piece of it uneaten. He saw footprints in the mud back behind the bushes leading into the woods, and someone had cut the branches to get a better view of the house. He didn't like it one bit. He didn't want to alarm her, so he pondered what to do. He decided that while she was with him, he would ask his best friend and roommate Troy Levy to take a closer look at the area surrounding Lucy's house.

Troy was a detective and crime scene investigator with the Maine State Troopers' office. He would be the right man for the job; he was better qualified since he was more experience in research and resources. Cole was mostly highway patrol investigations. He had met Troy at the Maine Police Academy several years back. They were in the same classes, and became buddies quickly. They were both stationed in Houlton, and decided to become work partners. Since they were both single men, they eventually ended up sharing a house. He trusted Troy to be discreet and detached.

***

Cole turned in the direction of the door to peek into the house. She was still busy packing, so he shouted, "Lucy, take your time; I have a call to make. I'll be right back." He heard her say, "Okay." He stepped off the porch and walked down the driveway to his bike. He reached down into one of the saddle-bags and took his cellphone out. Cole dialed the number, then scuffed the gravel under his feet as the phone rang.

"Hi, what's up?" Troy answered cheerfully, as he usually did. He was almost always in a good mood.

"Hey! I'm on my way home with Lucy. Are you going to be home? I have something I want to talk to you about—a favor to ask, really." Cole replied. He watched the front door as he spoke, waiting for Lucy to come out at any moment.

"Sure, anything! I'll be home," Troy answered.

"I think someone's been spying on Lucy from the woods, but I'm not sure. I can't talk now, so I'll explain when I get home. And let's keep this between us, at least until we know for certain," Cole said. He saw Lucy stepping out on the landing. She locked the door and headed his way.

"I have to go. I'll talk to you when we get there. I'll be there shortly," Cole told him, and hung up the phone. He dropped his cellphone back in the bag, then opened his arms wide as she approached, and held her as she snuggled on his chest.

"I'm all yours, to do with as you please," she joked.

Cole heard her giggle, and she slapped his butt. He kissed the top of her head and said, "Be careful what you wish for," then pulled her close and swatted her derriere. They both laughed. Cole mounted the bike, Lucy slipping her body behind his. She scooted closer, wrapped her arms around his torso, and he felt her lay her head on his shoulder. He started the engine and headed for his house.

Within ten minutes, Cole pulled into his driveway. Troy came to greet them at the door.

"Hi, guys," he yelled in their direction, stepping forward on the porch.

Cole had bought this older farmhouse two years ago, when he'd been stationed in Houlton and was searching for a place. It was built in the fifties, but the family that lived there before them had kept it in good condition. He instantly fell in love with the house. It was more than he wanted to pay for it, so Troy offered to become his roommate; it all worked out great. They got along, and they respected each other's space. The house still needed some work here and there, but nothing major. He liked all the original woodwork and the three fireplaces that helped with the heating bill, especially during the long winters.

"Hi, Troy, nice to see you again," Lucy replied as she approached him and waved at him. Cole trailed behind her. Cole's large German Shepherd, King, came running out from the side of the house and jumped up on Cole's chest. His tail wagged frantically.

"Down boy, we have company," he told the dog playfully.

"I'd like you to meet King," he said to Lucy, who was watching the dog with wide eyes.

"He's a beautiful dog," she answered, extending her hand cautiously to pet him. King just sat down next to her and nudged her leg.

"He likes you; otherwise he would bark. He's a trained K9 dog. I raised him since he was a puppy," Troy told her. They all entered the house and headed to the kitchen, the dog following close behind. Cole took Lucy's backpack and set it next to the door.

"Hey, we're going to barbecue and just chill for the afternoon, maybe go for a swim at Nickerson Lake. What about you?" Cole asked Troy. He opened the refrigerator door, reached in and took out two Coronas. "Want one?" he asked Troy.

"Sure." Cole grabbed another beer, opened all three and passed them around.

"It's such a nice day; why don't we sit outside on the veranda?" Lucy suggested, then sipped on her beer.

"That's a good idea. Come on, King. We're going outside," Cole said. He grabbed a bag of nacho chips and a jar of salsa from the cupboard. He placed them on a tray with napkins.

"Would you mind taking this out?" Cole asked Lucy. "I'll be right there. I just need to talk to Troy about work for a second."

"Sure, no problem," she answered. She picked up the tray and headed outside with King.

"Thanks, I won't be long," Cole said. He watched her and the dog leave the kitchen, waiting until she was out of earshot before he spoke another word.

Troy looked at him curiously. In a serious tone he asked, "What's up?"

"Listen, I'd like you to do me a favor. Someone delivered wildflowers to Lucy on her porch at night, twice. She thought they were from me at first, but..." Cole shook his head and continued, "She said she thought she saw someone in the bushes near the woods last night. I told her it was probably just an animal. But I went to look around, I found food wrappers and saw footprints. Whoever it was trimmed down the bushes to have direct sight of her house. Would you mind checking it out? It's just strange. I didn't say anything to her, because I didn't want to frighten her," Cole explained to Troy. He sighed, turning to glance at Lucy, who was sitting in the loveseat with her feet up on the railing.

"Sure, I'll go down and take a look. There are quite a few hiking trails near the lake. It could just be kids fooling around," Troy answered, then gulped down his beer.

"Thanks. Let me know what you find, okay? Let's keep this between us until we know more. It might be nothing. I don't want to scare her," Cole said. as he sipped his beer.

"I'll leave now since she's here," Troy said and walked out of the kitchen toward his car. Cole watched him leave, then turned around and went outside to sit beside Lucy on the love seat. He sat down, placing his hand on her knee, and asked, "So, what shall we barbecue—chicken or steaks?"

***

Troy headed toward New Limerick. He drove slowly up Lucy's long driveway and parked his car near the front entrance of the house. He stepped up on the veranda and took the few strides to the back of the bungalow. He saw the flowers on the rocking chair. He didn't touch them, but leaned down to examine them closer. Troy tilted his head as he determined if they were from the area. He had an idea where they might have been picked; there was a meadow not far from here that hosted a wide array of wildflowers. He turned around, lifted his hand to shield his eyes from the sun, and set his sight toward the bushes. He noticed what looked like a hole between the leaves and branches as he walked toward the area. He made a beeline toward the trees. Branches had obviously been cut with something sharp, probably some kind of scissors.

Troy pushed the small branches aside with one hand and took only one step forward, trying not to disturb anything. He saw that the high grass was crushed, pressed down to the ground in the area behind the opening, as if someone had been sitting there for some time. He scanned the ground, then moved a couple of paces to his left. Troy observed footprints, probably someone wearing boots, in the mud a yard away. He took his measuring tape out of his pocket, bent down and measured the length and width of the print, noting that it was half an inch in depth. He wrote down his findings in a small notebook.

Troy stood erect, his hands on his hips as he thought about a size ten shoe or boot. He computed the person who left the imprint should be about five feet five to seven inches tall, and weigh about one ninety to two hundred pounds. He shoved the notebook back into his pocket.

One step at a time, he followed the imprints looking for clues—until he lost the trail on a paved hiking path, which led to a park down the road. Troy sighed heavily as he looked both ways on the path. He didn't like what he'd found. He had no more leads, but he knew someone was definitely watching her. Cole wouldn't rest until he found out who it was and why. Troy slowly backtracked to Lucy's house.

He hurried back to home to find Cole and Lucy. As he entered, he could hear laughter coming from the backyard; he headed toward the sound. Cole was at the grill flipping burgers, and Lucy was trying to get him to give her the spatula. She kept reaching for it, and he kept pulling away as she giggled.

"Would you sit down over there and relax? I'm the chef!" Cole told her. He held the spatula over his head, and she jumped for it. Troy was grinning at them, watching their antics from the veranda.

"All right children, settle down," he yelled. They both stopped and laughed some more. Troy looked straight at Cole without any expression on his face.

"Would you like a burger?" Cole asked, as he flipped another one.

"I would love one, but I'm going to get another beer. Anyone else ready for another?" he asked. He discreetly leaned his head toward the kitchen to indicate he wanted Cole to follow him inside.

"I'll help you. Here, you can be the chef for a while," Cole extended the spatula to Lucy. She took it from him and made a face at him. He leaned forward and kissed her quickly before he marched up the steps.

The two men stood close together in the kitchen, in front of the refrigerator. Cole whispered, "So, what did you find out?" He peeked outside at Lucy, working the grill. Troy opened the fridge and passed him two beers.

"I found some footprints, and followed them to a trail about a quarter of a mile up in the woods. Judging by the prints I found, he's a not a big guy. *Someone* was unquestionably there. Who, I don't know. All I can tell you is that the footprints were fresh. I'd keep a close eye out, to see if he comes back," Troy filled Cole in between swallows of his beer.

"Shit! Now I'm kind of worried. I'll keep her here for the weekend, and think of something later. Don't mention anything," Cole instructed. Troy nodded.

"Thanks. Now, let's eat. I'm starving," Cole informed Troy, heading out the door to the backyard.

"You're always hungry," Troy retorted, as he followed him outside.

***

It was the end of a perfect day; Lucy was sitting on a wood swing observing the men as they cleaned the table. King had taken a liking to her, and kept shadowing her everywhere. Maybe it was because she had sneaked him bites of meat most of the afternoon. He lay next to her on the ground with his ear perked upward. She insisted on helping clean up, but the guys told her to go away since she had prepared the meal. She drank the last sip of her wine and placed the glass next to her.

"We're almost done. I'll be right there," Cole shouted to her, as he carried the last plate inside the house. She smiled as she thought about how lucky she was to have met him. He was considerate, kind...and she was falling in love with him. Cole came out of the house carrying another bottle of white wine in one hand and a beer in the other. She loved his broad shoulders, and she could distinguish his six-pack under his snug T-shirt as he moved closer to her.

"I noticed you didn't have any more wine, so..." he said, lifting the bottle in the air as he approached her. He snuggled beside her on the swing. He kissed her lightly on the mouth. "Mmm!" she heard him say.

"Are you trying to get me drunk and take advantage of me?" She teased him as she giggled. She'd already had too much to drink, but she was having such a good time. She was feeling tipsy. Cole poured her another half a glass, then she stopped him by pulling her glass upward.

"Enough! I don't want you to get the upper hand here," she joked and laughed. He reached over with his strong hands, lifted her, and pulled her over his knees. She embraced him around the neck with her free arm.

"I would never take advantage of you, but I really don't mind if you take advantage of me," he whispered in her ear, then nibbled on her earlobe.

"Maybe I will," Lucy responded. She moved her head and kissed him passionately. Their tongues dancing to each other's rhythms, she could feel an erection mounting underneath her. She heard another moan come from Cole. She pulled back and gazed at his beautiful face, then gently caressed the side of his cheek with her fingers.

"Let's go inside, unless you'd rather stay here," he suggested. Lucy nodded. Cole wrapped his hands under her legs and scooped her up. He stood with her in his arms and carried her straight to his bedroom, which was located at the end of the corridor on the first floor. He gently placed her on top of his bed, then stepped back and took his shirt off. *What a wonderful body,* she thought. She reached up and drew him closer to her as his fingers slowly unbuttoned her blouse, one at a time. His eyes were fixed on her, a sexy grin on his face. She leaned upward and enveloped her mouth with his, and...

***

At the break of dawn, the birds chirped so loudly they woke her. Lucy opened her eyes and looked toward the window, which was slightly open. She lay immobile next to her lover, thinking how much she loved him—and hoped he wouldn't break her heart. She moved her head to the right to admire him sleeping. *He looks so handsome and peaceful with his eyes closed,* she thought.

Lucy quietly slipped out of bed without waking him up. She tiptoed to the chair and picked up his T-shirt, inhaling his scent before she put it on. She then searched around for her bag, and found it next to the bedroom door. Lucy opened it and pulled on a pair of shorts, then headed to the kitchen. King must have heard her, because he rushed up to her with his tail wagging.

"Good morning, King," she told him as she petted his head. Troy was already up, sitting at the table having coffee and reading the newspaper. He was dressed in his state trooper uniform, ready for work.

"Good morning, Lucy. There's some coffee made, over there," he said, pointing to the pot on the counter. He folded his paper and placed it on the table, then stood up and took his last sip of coffee.

"Gotta go; have a nice day," he said, and walked away toward the front door.

"Thanks, see you later," she said. Lucy poured herself a cup of coffee and added cream. Grabbing the paper from the table on the way, she went to sit outside on the porch steps. King followed closely on her heels. He lay down beside her on the porch, sighing contentedly. She put her cup down beside her and began to read the paper. A half hour later, she heard footsteps. She looked up, and Cole was standing at the screen door with his own cup of coffee.

"Good morning; did you sleep well? I didn't hear you sneak out," he asked, and sat down near her. He gave her a peck on the cheek.

"You were sleeping so soundly, and I had company," she told him, reaching down to stroke King's head.

"Hey, King, you trying to steal my girl?" he joked. The dog's ears perked up and he looked up at Cole, but didn't budge from his spot.

"So what would you like to do today? I don't have to be at work until eight o'clock. I have the night shift tonight," Cole said to her as he sipped his coffee.

"I don't know what did you have in mind?" she asked as she eyed the fields by his house.

"I don't mind just hanging around the house. We don't have to do anything. We *could* return to bed; now that's a thought," he replied, and caressed her leg with his fingers. She placed her hand over his to stop him from going further up her thigh, beaming at him.

"Yes, we could...but, we are not. How about we pack a lunch, have a picnic and go to the lake for a swim this afternoon? You can drive me back home before work," she suggested in a sweet tone, then glanced up at him.

"That's perfect, and we still have the whole morning to ourselves," he teased once again then smirked at her. She slapped his arm lightly and stood up.

"Me and King are going to pack a lunch while you go shower, then I'll shower so we have time to spend at the lake. Now go," she ordered. Lucy blew a kiss at him then turned her head toward the door. "Get going!" she poked Cole in the side playfully.

"Ahh! Come on! Fine. Let's go, King," he said, but the dog just lay motionless next to her. King didn't move, not even his head. She patted the top of his head and giggled.

"Traitor," Cole said, as he glanced at the dog. They both laughed. He stood and went inside. She stroked King's back. "Good boy," she whispered near his ear.

An hour later, Lucy had packed up a bag and was ready to go to the lake. She had changed into a blue bikini and black cover-up. Cole came around the counter and whistled at her as she placed the last sandwich in a baggie. He wrapped his arms around her waist and pulled her close against his body. He kissed her lightly on the lips, then muttered in her ear, "Are you sure you want to go to the lake?" He then brushed his lips down her neck. Lucy shook her head then nodded as she sniggered. She gently pushed him away and said, "Let's go! We have lots of time for that later on. Come on, King! You are coming too." The dog barked and jumped up. He went to the door, sat down and waited. Cole picked up his keys from the counter and swung the strap of the bag over his shoulder.

"Okay, you win. You even have King on your side," he replied. and they walked to his truck with King following. Lucy opened the back door for King; the dog jumped in and immediately sat down in the back seat behind Cole. They drove to Sokosis Lake, another body of water nearby, where swimmers swamped the beach and enjoyed the picnic area. They parked in the public lot and walked down to the beach. Cole was holding on to King's leash and bag as Lucy led the way, carrying a large blanket. They walked along the edge of the water until they were almost at the end of the sandy area, where they found a private spot under a tree.

"How about here?" Lucy asked, pointing. Cole nodded, and she spread the blanket on the ground. The afternoon was hot, and time passed quickly. They swam, sunbathed, and ate. At three o'clock, they were packing up because Cole needed to get ready for work. He said, "Hey! Why don't you take King home with you? You seemed to get along so well; I'm sure Troy wouldn't mind. I have to work the overnight shift, and he could keep you company. I'll come by in the morning."

Lucy looked down at the dog and asked, "You want to come home with me, boy?" The dog just wagged his tail as if he understood.

"Well, sure that would be great," she answered Cole. They strolled back to the truck hand in hand. About a half hour later, Cole parked at the end of her driveway and kissed her goodbye. Lucy waved to him as he disappeared down the road. She unlocked her door and went inside. King followed her with no prompting.

"Here we are, King. Make yourself at home." He just lay down on the rug by the door. She figured he must be tired from running around at the beach. Lucy opened the icebox and took out a pound of hamburger meat to cook for King later on. She didn't have any dog food, so hamburger meat would do. She walked to the bathroom to take a quick shower. She untied her bikini top and bottom, letting them fall to the floor, and stepped under the hot water.

Refreshed by her shower, Lucy dressed in a pair of shorts and a tank top. She headed in the direction of the kitchen. *King must be hungry*, she thought. He hadn't budged from his spot by the door. She opened a bottle of Pinot grigio and poured herself a glass to sip as she cooked the meat for King's supper. When it was ready, she placed it in a bowl and grabbed her wine in the other hand. She looked down at the K9; King had moved closer to her from his spot by the door, probably due to the smell of the food. He was waiting eagerly for his food, sitting with an alert expression and watching her closely.

"How about we go sit outside? It's such a beautiful day," she said, walking toward the back door. She pushed the screen door open and placed the bowl on the porch. He immediately came forward and ate the whole meal within seconds. When he finished, he lay down next to her as she rocked in her rocking chair. A half hour later, she was gazing out on the water, sipping her wine and reminiscing about the wonderful time she and Cole had. She petted King frequently; it was nice to have his company. Suddenly the dog sat up; his ears perked up, and he growled at something as he looked toward the bushes at the end of the yard.

"There's nothing there King; it's probably just a squirrel. Stay!" Lucy said calmly. He just snarled again. She jumped in her chair when the dog started to bark. She was afraid he might take off running in the direction of the woods after the critters, and she might lose him, so she held his collar as she spoke to him softly.

"There's nothing there, King. Shh!" she said, as she stroked the top of his head gently. He kind of quieted down, but he growled a little. Lucy decided to take him inside. She stood up, still holding on to his collar tightly, and virtually dragged him inside.

"Come *on*, King. Inside!" she barked, when he resisted her orders.

Chapter 7

Rodney took his daily walk to Lucy's after he had finished work. He whistled most of the way, anticipating seeing her again. He had come by yesterday, but she wasn't there. He'd waited for her for a few hours, then gave up. She had been on his mind all day. As he approached his hiding place behind the bushes, he crouched down, not wanting to be seen. He was careful where he stepped, avoiding the noise of twigs snapping.

Lucy was sitting on the porch, drinking a glass of wine. She was so beautiful! He noticed her bare shoulders and her long, bare legs up on the railing. There was a dog lying next to her. He thought, *Who's dog is that?* He hadn't seen a dog before. *Maybe she bought a dog.* He stirred a bit to get a better view. Rodney was startled when he saw the dog sit up and look his way. The dog barked a few times, and then growled menacingly.

Rodney didn't move a muscle, afraid the dog might come charging at him. He wasn't attached to a leash. He watched as Lucy bent down to talk to the dog softly, then grabbed his collar to take him inside. Rodney wanted to hear her soothing voice. He reached up and touched his ear as the wind blew his hair away from it. He waited, hoping she would return outside, but she didn't. *Damn dog, now she's gone.* He would have to do something about that dog. Rodney stayed for another hour, watching her through the windows as she went from one room to another.

As he sat, his mind drifted to what she might be wearing under her clothing and what she wore to bed. He licked his lips as he observed her from afar. His hand slipped down to his crotch area to touch a mounting erection. He liked the sensation; it was something he'd seldom experienced before he met her. He crawled away from his hiding spot and backed away. He walked cautiously to his right, following the bushes against the tree line, making sure not to be seen. He stopped behind the larger trees where he might be able to get a better view of her through her bedroom window, but it wasn't meant to be. He removed his backpack and reached inside for his binoculars. He didn't have them; he'd left them on the table at his house. He would have to return home, a mile and a half away.

Rodney was furious with himself, and he punched the bag several times. "God Damn it!" he said out loud. He gripped the bag in his hand tightly and walked away. He angrily kicked the pebbles down his path as he trudged back to his house. *I will come back after dark*, he thought, *and I'll be able to watch her better with the lights inside.*

Rodney arrived at the old farmhouse and grabbed the doorknob, swung open the back door with enough force to bounce it off the wall and leave a dent. He didn't bother to close it. He was still annoyed with himself. He marched inside and flopped into one of the chairs in the living room. He scanned the room, disgusted that he had to leave her because he really couldn't see her very well. He jumped up and ran to his bedroom. He tossed clothes to the side then hurled empty boxes behind him as he searched his bedroom. He stood up and looked around the room. Glancing toward the side of the dresser, he observed three large boxes. He dug into them, taking everything out.

"Where the fuck is it?" he asked as he tossed one box to his right side. He plowed into the next one, sweat appearing on his brow from frustration at not finding what he was searching for. Finally, when he opened the last carton, he sat back on his heels and smirked at what he saw. *Finally! There it is*, he thought. *I'll be able to get nice photos now.* It was a long lens camera his grandmother had used to bird watch in the parks when she was alive. It was her prized possession. He cradled it in his hands and looked at it for a moment before standing up to walk back to the living room, placing it on the coffee table. A smile appeared as he thought about Lucy. He would be able to take closer, more defined pictures with this camera. *Why didn't I remember this before? This is much better than the binoculars.*

Rodney sat down next to the table and studied the camera. He wished he had the instruction manual, but he didn't have time to read it anyway. Looking out the living room window, he saw the sun was going down. It would take him a half hour to get back to Lucy's bungalow. He wanted to see her before she went to bed. He hurried to his closet in his bedroom and changed clothes, dressing all in black. He pulled his black wool cap down low and walked into the kitchen.

He put the camera into his backpack, grabbed a bottle of water from the fridge and headed back out to find his princess. Rodney followed the path until he came to the crossroads and took a left into the woods toward the lake. He crouched down as he approached the edge. He could see the lights were on. Sitting on the ground, Rodney swung his backpack in front of him and took out the camera. He took out the biggest lens, attached it, and brought it up to his eye. Rodney smiled as he watched her; he could see her much better now, and take pictures of her close up. He wanted to get closer, but he wondered about the dog. *Will the dog bark to let her know I'm near her house?* He decided to wait a bit.

He watched intently for another half an hour. Lucy talked on the phone, moving from room to another. Rodney couldn't help himself; he had to get closer to the windows. He gathered his bag and swung it on his back. Holding his camera tightly in his right hand, he pushed forward cautiously. His eyes darted from left to right with every step he took toward the house. He squatted down low as he approached the large window. He leaned his back flat against the siding of the house. Rodney's heart pounded in his chest with excitement and nervousness at the same time; he was afraid she might catch him. He waited silently as he regained his composure.

Rodney poked his head up to the rim of the window frame and peeked inside. He didn't see her, but the dog was right there, lying down by the back door. He scanned the room quickly, and lifted his camera to be ready when she would come in. Suddenly the dog sat up, then sprinted to the window barking furiously. All Rodney saw was the dog's teeth flashing as it barked, and its eyes riveted on him. He jerked back so the animal couldn't see him. The sounds of the dog's howling made him scurry for cover, back to the edge of the woods. He got on his knees down behind the bushes, his heart racing faster than he ever thought it could.

His eyes fixed on the bungalow, he tried to calm down. He stared in horror as Lucy opened the back door and let the dog out. The large German Shepherd bolted toward his position. He heard Lucy yell, "King! Come back here, King!" Rodney stood, turned, and scampered as fast as he could in the direction of the trails to return home. Through the bushes and tall grass, he ran with all his might. He looked back and saw the dog was fifty feet away, heading straight for him, not slowing down. The dog had an aggressive growl; his bared teeth were still showing. A feeling of panic and dread passed through Rodney as he felt a cold sweat start to run down his back. Every step he took, it seemed the dog was getting closer. Rodney lost the race when his foot got lodged between two vines that were sticking out of the ground. He felt his foot twist, and tried to cushion his fall as he toppled over onto the wet ground.

He turned over onto his back just as the animal lunged on top of him. He raised his left forearm to shield his face just in time; the dog dug his fierce teeth into the fabric of his jacket, all the way through to his skin. Rodney screamed from the pain of the bite as the dog shook his head from side to side. He could hear the dog's growl and feel his skin rip. He punched the dog in the head several times, but its grip was still secure. He swept his right hand around on the ground beside him, trying to feel for something—anything—to defend himself with, as the agony increased in his arm. Rodney turned his head to the side briefly, and saw a rock about three feet away. *If only I can reach it*, he thought. He extended his arm, stretched as far as he could, and pushed his body with his feet toward the rock. His fingers were barely touching it. He shifted his body a little closer. His fingers dug into the dirt as they wrapped around the stone, embedded in the mud. He gripped it tightly, raised his hand, and brought several quick blows down with deadly force on the side of the dog's head.

Finally, the dog loosened his grip and let go of his arm, squealing loudly. It then collapsed on the ground next to him. Rodney sighed heavily. He pressed his hand on his arm to stop the bleeding; his wound was now bleeding through his jacket. He applied pressure to it and sat up, then pushed himself away from the dog. Rodney picked up his camera, which lay beside him broken into pieces. He stood, still dazed from the animal's assault. Rodney looked at the bloody animal on the ground one last time, then limped away toward his house while holding his arm.

***

Lucy stood on the back porch, her hands on the railing, afraid to go any further after she heard the agonizing cries of King in the woods. She rubbed her arms, but not because of the cold; it was the uncertainty, the unknown, that gave her chills. She scanned the area, but couldn't see anything in the darkness. It was dead silent. A frigid shiver passed down her back. She was petrified of what might have happened to King. She whirled, fumbled with the doorknob for a second, and went inside. She immediately locked the door and ran to find her cellphone. She searched blindly, glancing back at the door. When she found her phone, Lucy dialed Cole's number. She tapped her foot on the floor wildly as she waited for him to answer.

"Cole? Cole, something's wrong! I'm afraid," she said between gasping breaths. Lucy held the phone tightly to her ear while keeping her eye on the door.

"Lucy, calm down. Tell me what's wrong," he said calmly.

"King was barking, so I let him out, and then...he...he..." she said as tears started to fall down her cheeks. She cried, trying to speak between sobs.

"Lucy, are you all right? Are you hurt?" he questioned.

"I'm okay, but I don't know what happened to King. He ran toward the back woods, then I heard him screech, and...and he didn't come back. I don't know what to do. Please, come," she replied as she wept quietly.

"Lucy, I'm on my way. I want you to lock the doors and stay inside. Do you hear me? Do not open the door to anyone. Do you understand?" he instructed in a stern tone.

"Yes, I understand. I did that. What's going on?" she asked.

"Just stay inside. I'll be there in less than ten minutes," he replied, and she heard the click of his phone. He had hung up. Lucy looked at her cellphone blankly. What was happening? Something was going on that she didn't know about, and she definitely was not going to budge from her spot. She stood in the kitchen with her back to the wall. She darted away from the wall briefly to yank open a drawer and take a knife out; Lucy gripped the handle tightly while she waited for the unknown. Her eyes kept returning to the clock across the room on the wall. The seconds ticked away slowly; every minute seemed like an hour. Beads of cold sweat appeared on her forehead, and her lower lip trembled with fright. Her eyes darted back and forth from the windows to the doors. *Where are you, Cole? Please hurry!*

Ten minutes went by before she finally heard the siren of a cop car. She sighed a breath of relief, but still didn't budge from her place against the wall. The sound of the siren got closer, and she noticed blue lights outside reflecting on the walls. Lucy ran to the door with the knife still in her hand. She waited nervously by the door before she unlocked it, her anticipation to hear Cole's voice growing by the second. Her whole body shook until she heard his voice.

"Lucy! It's me, open the door," Cole called out. She saw him run up the porch steps two at a time. She grabbed the doorknob and swung the door open, and Cole immediately swaddled her in his arms. Tears began to fall from relief that he was there. She was finally safe. Her whole body was shaking uncontrollably. He held her so tight she could barely catch her breath, and she could feel his heart pounding against her chest. He took the knife from her hand and placed it on the table.

"It's all right. I'm here, don't cry," Cole told her as he kissed the top of her head. He held her for a minute as she tried to get her emotions in check.

"Something happened to King. He ran out to the back yard, and he didn't come back. I heard him cry out," she blurted out, still not letting him go. They walked toward the living room.

"Okay, I want you to sit here on the couch and not move. I'm going to go see if I can find him," he told her. He kissed her on the cheek. There was no way she was going to stay put. She grabbed his hand and glanced up at him with tears in her eyes.

"No, I'm coming with you. I don't want to be alone," she insisted. He nodded. They walked to the back door. Cole scanned the yard from the door. He took his gun out of its holster and held it ready beside him.

"I want you to follow me, and stay behind me. Do you understand?" Cole said, gripping the doorknob. Lucy nodded. Her heart started to race once more as she took the first few steps on the porch. He motioned for her to be quiet by lifting his finger and placing it on his lips. She gestured in agreement by inclining her head. They moved forward toward the wooded area, her hand touching his back for reassurance. When they approached the high grass, he raised his gun in front of him and held his flashlight in the other hand. Lucy gasped, frightened.

Why does he need a gun? Was there someone there?

"Be quiet; not a word," he whispered. They took a few steps forward, walking into the woods trying to be quiet and cautious like rodents. She listened to every sound of their surroundings. Cole stopped and turned his head to his right. She could hear a faint whimper coming from that direction. They moved cautiously between the bushes and the trees; the sound was growing stronger as they moved forward. Cole's light illuminated the area until he spotted an object on the ground. Lucy was behind him, so she moved to the side to see what he had found. It was King. Cole marched to him, bent down and gently touched him. He lay motionless on the wet ground. Cole turned his head from side to side, examining his surroundings.

"Oh, my God! He's hurt," Lucy exclaimed quietly as she saw the blood running down from his head. Cole handed the flashlight to her, and put his gun away. He picked up King in his arms and took a last look around.

"Let's get out of here," he said. Cole led the way, almost running back to the bungalow through the woods carrying King. Lucy followed closely. She was confused and in disbelief. *How did he get hurt? An animal must have attacked him.* Cole didn't speak until he placed King on the porch. Lucy noticed tears pooling in his eyes.

"Go get me a towel, and hurry. We need to take him to the hospital, but first I need to try and stop the bleeding," he said, concerned. Lucy glanced at King and saw he had a large gash by his brow. She heard the dog whimper, and it broke her heart. Guilt invaded her whole body. She shouldn't have let him out. The front of Cole's uniform shirt was bloody from carrying the dog.

Lucy heard Cole say, "It's okay, King I'm here." She rushed as fast as she could to the bathroom and grabbed two beach towels. She hurried back to give them to Cole. He bundled the dog's head securely, slipped his hands under King once again, and lifted him up in his arms. Cole carried him to his squad car and carefully laid him the backseat. Lucy sat beside him and stroked his body with a shaking hand. Cole raced back around the car to the driver's seat. He started the police car and backed out of her driveway with the siren on and lights flashing, leaving a trail of dust behind him.

Chapter 8

Cole's heart thumped hard in his chest, and his hands sweated from nervousness. He still held the steering wheel securely, though, as he maneuvered his way to the only veterinary hospital in Houlton, passing numerous vehicles along the way. He called ahead to let them know he was coming with an injured K9 dog. He then radioed Troy, so he could meet them at the clinic. *Whoever hurt his dog will pay dearly; if King died...* Cole thought. *Stop thinking that way. He's going to be just fine.* Cole kept repeating this in his thoughts.

It had seemed an eternity before he pulled into the driveway of the animal hospital. The veterinarian waited for him in the lobby with a gurney and a nurse. Cole jammed the brakes, gravel flying. He jumped out of the front seat and opened the back door of the cruiser without a word. He picked up King in his arms again, and within a few long strides he gently placed him on the stretcher. He stood motionless with his hands by his sides, watching them run away inside with King. He felt a soft hand touch his back.

"Come on, let's go in. He's going to be fine; he's in good hands now. He's a strong dog," he heard Lucy say as she rubbed his back. They followed the vet inside to a small trauma room, where they stood and watched as the vet treated King. He felt Lucy's hand intertwine in his. He turned his head and gave her a weak smile. Another siren was faintly heard moments later; it was Troy. Cole sighed heavily and bowed his head low as he thought how bravely King had guarded Lucy against the asshole who had injured him.

"Doc, what do you think? Is he going to make it?" Cole asked. His voice trembled a bit. Lucy squeezed his hand lightly.

"Well, he has a bad concussion, and a deep cut that I can sew up, but he lost a lot of blood. I can tell by the pale color of his gums. I need to get him to CAT scan and x-ray, then we will know better what's going on. He'll also need a blood transfusion. You might as well have a seat and get a cup of coffee; it's going to be a while. He's a fighter, Cole. Don't worry. He'll make it," the doctor said with confidence.

Cole felt a tug on his hand, "Let's sit down and wait. There nothing we *can* do, but wait. He's in good hands," Lucy said softly. She led him toward the waiting area. Cole didn't object; he just nodded. He was glad she was safe and by his side in this time of hardship. They walked down the hall. He slumped into a chair next to the entry door, bowed his head, and covered his face.

"Whoever did this will pay! I'll make sure of it," he told her gritting his teeth with anger.

"Who? What are you talking about?" Lucy asked. Cole noticed she was pale; Lucy had turned white as a sheet. Cole took her hands in his. He had to tell her the truth before Troy arrived. He couldn't call it a suspicion any longer.

"Listen, I don't want you to be alarmed, but Troy and I think someone has been stalking you from the edge of the trees for a while. We found food wrappers, footprints, and someone cut an opening by the bushes so he could observe you. We weren't a hundred percent sure, and that's why I wanted you to take King—to defend you," Cole said.

Lucy's mouth fell open in surprise. Her eyes bulged out in horror. Her hands and legs started to shake. Cole draped his arm around her shoulders and pulled her close to his chest. He stroked her hair softly.

"What are you telling me? Someone is... What am I going to do? Who... who is he?" Lucy asked with fright.

She's going to faint. She's so pale, he thought. "Troy is already on it. We will find him. You can stay with us until we find him, okay? Don't worry! It's okay. Please, don't cry," Cole told her. Tears rolled down her cheeks.

Suddenly the sound of the front glass doors opening got their attention. It was Troy bursting through the doors. Troy's strides were long, his face twisted in anger, and his brows were squeezed together from concern. His hands were balled into fists.

"How's he doing?" Troy asked Cole, placing his hand on Cole's shoulder. Cole lifted his head to look at him.

"He has a bad cut on his head, and a concussion. He lost a lot of blood. The doc took him to get x-rays and a CAT scan," he informed him.

"Are you all right, Lucy?" Troy asked, and sat next to her.

"I'm fine, thank you. I just pray King will be okay," she answered. She sat up and raised her hand to wipe the tears off of her face.

"Troy, I'm going to stay here and wait for the results of King's tests. Could you find out what is being done to get this asshole? Has the investigation team been called? What did they find?" Cole questioned in an urgent tone.

"The team is on the scene looking for evidence and clues. They called Jim to bring his dog in to try to track the bastard, but it just started to rain, so they don't know how long they can track. You know sometimes you lose the trail when it rains. The guys are out in the streets, on the lookout for anyone who might need treatment for a dog bite. King must have had a good grip on him, if he had to hit him hard enough to give him a concussion," Troy answered and glanced toward the trauma room.

"We'll get him. He'll pay for this, believe me, he'll pay," Troy added. He stood and started to pace the floor in front of them. His white-knuckled fists gripped his utility belt. Cole knew he was furious at the monster who had hurt King; they both loved him. The three of them had lived together in the same house for years.

"Troy, we have to play it cool if we want to catch him. Otherwise, we might lose him. He knows we're on to him, so we don't want him to flee," Cole advised him seriously. He rose to stand beside Troy, then touched his arm gently to stop his pacing.

"Troy, have a seat and keep Lucy company while I check on King. It's been forty-five minutes. How long can x-rays take?" Cole asked.

"Sorry, man! Sure, you go ahead. I'll be here. I'll hold the fort," Troy replied. He gave Cole a small smile, and sat down next to Lucy. He patted her knee in reassurance. Troy didn't say a word, but they seemed to understand each other's pain. Cole walked down the corridor, glancing from right to left until he found the doctor in one of the rooms with King. He approached the large cage that King lay in. The dog had a needle bandaged to his leg, and was getting a blood transfusion.

"I sedated him. He'll need to be observed closely for the next day or so. He was lucky there were no fractures. Everything else looks good. If you want, I'll stay with him for the night. There isn't much you can do here. Go home, and I'll call you if he gets worse," he informed Cole with a smile.

"Thanks a lot, Doc. You have my number. I'll be home. Troy or I will be taking a few days off from work to care for him," Cole said and shook his hand. Cole was grateful King would be in good hands. He went to tell Lucy and Troy.

When Lucy saw him, she stood up immediately. "How is he?" she asked. She bit her lower lip, waiting anxiously for his answer.

"He's getting a transfusion; no skull fractures, though, and the doc gave him a tranquilizer. Doc's optimistic, and he told us to go home. He'll call if anything changes," Cole told them. He saw Lucy bow her head, speechless. He knew she was blaming herself for King's injuries.

"Lucy, it wasn't your fault, so stop feeling guilty. You are coming home with me until we find that bastard, okay? Troy, keep me up to date on what you find," Cole said and grabbed Lucy's hand. She seemed more at ease at now, even though she wasn't saying much. Troy nodded, then left them to go check on King.

"Come on, let's go home," Cole said, and led Lucy back to his cruiser.

***

Rodney was furious about the mishap with the dog. *How careless I was! I should have left when I saw the dog. I wouldn't be hurting now*, he thought. He could hear police sirens in the distance, headed his way. He pulled hard on the bottom of his shirt until he ripped off a large piece, big enough to wrap his wound. He tied it tightly, making a rough knot. He put pressure on the wound on his arm to try to stop the bleeding seeping through the makeshift bandage. His arm was throbbing with pain. Rodney winced, but not just from the discomfort; he knew he was leaving a blood trail, but what could he do? Walking toward the path, he was relieved when he felt droplets of rain falling on his face. He trudged through the bushes and trees until he reached the path back to his house. Rodney smirked as the rain intensified. He knew that the police would not be able to follow his scent or detect the blood; the rain would wash it all away. *They will not catch me,* he thought and laughed out loud. *I was lucky today, but next time I will be prepared for anything, even a fucking dog,* he thought.

He quickened his pace when he saw the farmhouse appear through the trees. Another few yards and he would be back in the comfort of his house. He stepped up the last tread onto his porch, swung open the door and entered. He marched directly to the bathroom, where he finally could examine his arm. Rodney unwrapped his bandage, then pulled his jacket off and gingerly rolled his sleeve up. The dog's teeth had punctured several holes in his forearm, and a piece of flesh had ripped away to hang in a flap. He was fortunate that it wasn't any worse. It could be fixed, and would heal in time. He didn't dare go to the hospital, afraid the cops might be searching for someone with a dog bite. Rodney washed the dirt and blood from his wounds with soap and water, then he wrapped his arm in a clean towel and put pressure on it.

Rodney put a bottle of Tylenol in his pocket, then walked to the kitchen and found the duct tape in one of the drawers. He wrapped a solid layer of tape over the towel. Rodney finally took a glass from the cupboard and poured water into it. He took the Tylenol out of his pocket, popped three pills into his mouth and washed them down with a gulp of water. Next, he headed to the living room where he lay down on the couch. An hour later he was sound asleep, and had not even bothered to change his clothes.

The next morning, he woke up at dawn. His arm didn't hurt as badly as it had the night before. Rodney knew he had to show up for work. He got up and took off the old towel. He found a small clean dishcloth, ripped it in two, and folded it over his wound. He fastened it up with tape again. It wouldn't be as bulky as the towel. He decided he would go to the pharmacy on his lunch hour to pick up antibiotic cream and bandages.

Rodney went to the closet and took out a clean shirt and pants. After he dressed, he walked out of the house as if nothing happened. He picked up his bike, which was propped against the wall, then he hopped on it and pedaled to work. Rodney arrived at the garage right on time, as he did every morning, and began his usual chore of sweeping the bays.

The morning passed quickly, since it was a long weekend; lots of people were traveling to visit relatives, and needed fuel for their cars. He was in the last garage bay when he noticed Lucy's SUV pull in for gas at one of the pumps. His eyes fixed on her, and he stopped to stare at his darling. Rodney stood perfectly still holding the broom, just mesmerized by her beauty. Her hair was up in a ponytail, and she wore a pair of dark sunglasses. He yelled out into the garage, "I've got it." He wiped his hands on his hips as he walked to the full-service gas pump. He grinned as he approached the truck. *She came to see me, how sweet*, he thought.

"Hi, Lucy. What can I do for you?" he asked cheerfully as he glanced at her. Then he saw another person sitting next to her. A man. Heat rose to his face, but he managed a small smile. A wave of jealousy came over him. This man's fingers were touching her arm. He couldn't see his face, so Rodney bent down near her window to see who the man was. *It's a trooper! What's his name? What's he doing with her?* he thought. *I need to stay calm.*

"Hi, Rodney. You can fill it up, please," she told him. She turned back to look at Cole. Rodney nodded, then took two steps toward the back of the Range Rover. He unscrewed the cap, unhooked the pump, pushed the button for the premium grade and started to dispense her gas. Rodney observed her closely, never taking his eyes off her. As Lucy looked at Cole, he gently touched her hair. *Don't touch her!* Rodney thought. *She belongs to me! Keep your hands off of her!* He grimaced at the man behind his cap. Rodney cast his sight away from the trooper for a moment, a brief respite from the hate that was building inside him.

Rodney stepped back and noticed a large gray duffle bag and suitcase on the backseat. Thoughts were racing through his head. *Where is she going? Or is it where are they going?* He felt a tightness grip his chest. Another wave of jealousy passed through him. *She's mine! Mine only!* Rodney had to find out where they were going. He pulled the nozzle out of the gas tank, replaced the cap, and placed the hose back in the pump. He turned and casually went back to the driver's window.

"That will be thirty-two dollars, Lucy. Are you going somewhere? I saw you had a bag packed. I hope it's better weather than this rain," he said. He acted as relaxed and unconcerned as he could muster. He did not make eye contact with her and lifted his hand up to the sky. "It looks like more rain."

"Yes, we are going to Moncton, New Brunswick, just for the weekend. I hope we have good weather. Here's thirty-five dollars," Lucy said and handed him the cash.

"I'll be right back with your change," he replied. He walked back inside to the office for her change all the while wondering where she was staying. He thought, *Should I ask? She'll tell me if he is going with her.*

"Thirty-two, pump one," he told the cashier, who made change for him. He glanced out the window. Rodney narrowed his eyes at the trooper through the glass, wishing it were he who was going with her. *She's so beautiful, so sweet. She will be mine!* he thought.

"Rodney, Rodney!" He heard his name being yelled. Rodney had been lost in his thoughts, and hadn't heard the cashier trying to hand him the change. He was in his own world and had forgotten where he was for just a minute.

"Sorry," he answered and grasped the cash. He returned to the vehicle as fast as he could. He handed the bills to Lucy.

"I hope you have a nice place to stay in Moncton," he mentioned casually.

"Yes, Cole booked a nice hotel called Beausejour," she replied and turned on the ignition. Rodney stepped back and said, "Have fun." He stood frozen on the spot until the vehicle was no longer in sight. His hands were balled into fists, the knuckles white from resentment and envy. Rodney's thoughts were racing. *I am going to find that hotel where they're staying. He can't have her! She belongs to me.* Walking back to the last bay he had to sweep, Rodney decided he needed to take a few days off from work. That was the only way he could find her. He needed a few days of vacation.

He told his boss he wanted the weekend off, and he left early. Rodney pedaled his bike as fast as he could back to the house, and ran straight to his grandmother's room. He and his grandmother had gone to Canada about seven years ago, before she had gotten sick. He walked to her dresser, opened the top drawer and pulled out every item out. He was throwing everything on the floor in a pile without concern. *No passport? Where could it be?* Next he rushed to the closet, where a bunch of boxes were stacked in the corner. One by one he emptied them, until finally, he found a large yellow envelope. He shoved his hand into it, taking all the items out. There it was! His passport. He checked the expiration date. He smirked, and licked the drool off his lower lip. It still had two years before the expiration date. He hurried to his room, yanked a duffel bag from the hall hook and grabbed a sweatshirt, two T-shirts, and two pairs of pants from around the room, shoving them into the bag. Rodney picked up a set of keys from the bowl on the side table, glanced down at them and said a silent prayer, hoping the truck would start. He didn't even bother to lock up the house. Rodney sprinted toward the red '99 Ford truck, which had been sitting in the barn since his grandfather's death. It was in good condition, and once he got it started, it would take him where he needed to go.

Chapter 9

Just an hour before they departed, the doctor gave them the news that King was out of danger. He would be fine, and he only needed to rest a couple of days. There wasn't anything he needed, they couldn't do anything more for King, and not to worry anymore. So Cole called in a favor and took the weekend off. Lucy was excited to spend more time with him.

Lucy drove past the Canadian border crossing and picked up the Trans-Canada highway toward the city of Moncton. She tapped her fingers on the steering wheel to the beat of an Elton John song, *Rocket Man*. She felt happy. She was with the man she was having deeper feelings for, and he was her protector.

"Are you hungry yet? I sure could use some food," Cole said, rubbing his stomach. She turned the music down. There was an Irving Service Station ahead that featured a truck stop restaurant.

"Sure, I could have a bite," she answered, clicked on her right blinker and turned into the parking lot. She really was in need of food since they had entered Canada. She felt weak and a little nauseous. *Maybe some nourishment will help*, she thought. She turned the wheel sharply and parked the SUV. They stepped out of the truck and walked to the restaurant area hand in hand. Lucy pulled her hand gently from his as they approached the steps of the entrance; she had spotted the restrooms sign.

"I need to use the ladies room. You go ahead, I'll be right back," she said, and gave him a weak smile.

"Sure, I'll get a table," he answered her.

"I'll be right back," she managed to say, and walked away as fast as she could, her hand on her belly. She definitely did not feel right, but she figured maybe it was from all the events that had been going on the past few days. She hoped she would feel better when they got to their destination. They only had about another half hour of driving, at the most. She entered the bathroom and went directly to the sink. She turned on the cold faucet, cupped water in her hands and splashed it on her face several times. It felt cool and refreshing. *I'm just tired*, she thought. She wiped her face and returned to the restaurant feeling a little better. She sat down next to Cole and grabbed the menu off the table.

"Anything good?" she asked as she took a sip of water.

"I think I'll have fish and chips. What about you?" Cole asked, as he closed the menu and glanced her way.

"I'm not too hungry. I'll have the chicken noodle soup and crackers," she replied. Lucy noticed the waitress approaching to take their order. The food came quickly. They ate and chatted about their plans. She was feeling better by the time they left the restaurant.

As they neared the truck, Lucy asked, "Do you mind driving for a while? I'd like to rest my eyes for a bit." Cole extended his hand and rubbed her arm.

"Sure. You feeling all right?" He came closer and pulled her against him, gave her a hug, and kissed the base of her neck. She wrapped her arms around his waist.

"I'm fine, just a little tired," she answered. He let go of her and took the keys.

"Okay, just checking," he told her. He hopped in and sat in the driver's seat. She made herself cozy by resting her head back, and closed her eyes as she listened to the soft music on the radio. She fell asleep within minutes.

The next thing she knew, Lucy felt a hand kneading her leg. She opened her eyes and blinked several times as she heard Cole say, "Wake up Sleepyhead, we're here." He parked in front of the hotel.

"Did you have a good nap?" he asked. Lucy stretched her arms forward. Dusk had fallen, and the city lights were shining brightly on the street. Lucy nodded.. She felt revived from the catnap.

"You should have woken me up earlier," she answered. She saw a man in a uniform coming near her SUV. He opened the passenger door and smiled at them.

"Welcome to Beausejour Hotel," he said. Lucy grabbed her pocketbook and straightened her blouse, smoothing out the wrinkles. Cole stepped out of the truck, opened the back, and took out their bags. Lucy got out and stood by the passenger door watching the bellhop put their suitcases on a trolley. Cole passed the valet the keys to park the vehicle. After a brief conversation, they were on their way. Cole went forward, and she followed him quietly as they entered the reception area.

Ten minutes later the front desk personnel had issued them their keys, and they were entering their room on the eighth floor. Lucy walked over to the window and pushed the curtains back to look at the city view. "Nice," she said. She felt Cole's hand running down her back like a feather, all the way to her butt. He pushed her hair to the side and kissed the nape of her neck. Lucy grinned as a shiver of lust invaded her body. She slowly turned to face him, her arms surrounding his midsection as her hands crept under his shirt. Their eyes fixed on each other. She lifted up on her tiptoes so she could reach his lips. Their tongues whirled together in rhythm. She pulled away slightly from his kiss and at that moment, without thinking, she whispered, "I love you." Cole's lips came crashing down on hers. He bent down and wrapped his arms around her, lifted her up and placed her on the king size bed, kissing her passionately.

***

Cole opened his eyes the next morning content to be by the side of the woman he was falling in love with. Her hair was disheveled from the night of lovemaking; her arm lay lightly on his stomach. He looked at her sleeping face and grinned to himself as he remembered the words she'd uttered the previous night: "I love you."

Could it be he had finally found the soul mate he'd been looking for all these years? Cole didn't want to admit it, but the last few weeks with this woman had been glorious. He never thought he would find a person he desired to spend the rest of his life within such a short time, but it was true. He did love her, with all his heart. He never wanted her to leave his side again. She was different from the other women he had dated in the past. She was always happy to see him, kind, humble, and he liked the way she made him feel: passionate, and loved.

Cole gently took her arm and placed it next to her. He quietly slipped out of bed and put on his shorts, then took three long strides to grip the doorknob. Turning, he slowly took one last peek at her before closing the bedroom door. He went to the living room of their suite and sat down on the chair next to the window, and put his feet up on the ottoman. Cole heard his stomach growl. He was always hungry lately. *It must be all the lovemaking,* he thought, and chuckled. He glanced at the clock on the wall; it was ten o'clock. He couldn't recall the last time he'd slept that late without an interruption from work.

Cole decided to surprise Lucy with breakfast in bed. He picked up the menu for room service and scanned through it. When he called, a cheerful woman came on the line.

"Good morning! Room service, how may I help you?"

"Hello, I'd like to place an order. This is room 823. I would like two omelets with ham and cheese, a basket of pastries, and a pot of coffee," he told her. He looked toward the bedroom door, hoping Lucy wouldn't wake up yet.

"Thank you. Will there be anything else?" she inquired pleasantly.

"No, that will be all, thank you," he answered, and hung up the phone. On the coffee table was a brochure of the activities in the area. Cole leafed through it to pass the time while waiting for the food, He noticed an advertisement about the Lobster Festival that was being held in Shediac. It was located about ten miles east of their location, and it might be fun to check out. There was also a lobster dinner, a carnival, and a band playing under a tent in the evening. It would be a short drive, and take care of the whole day. They could be like children, riding the rides and eating cotton candy. He would suggest it to Lucy when she woke up.

He rested his head against the back of the chair and closed his eyes as his mind wandered back to Lucy. He thought about how he loved to hear her giggle, how she would always shy away from his eyes when she was naked, and would cover herself up. *How delightful she was!* He was always happy when he was near her. Cole opened his eyes when he heard a noise coming from the bedroom. The door opened, and she was standing in the doorway, holding a sheet wrapped around her body. She tilted her head and smiled at him. A sexual feeling passed through his body. She looked so seductive, and he wanted to take her at that precise moment.

"Hey there, Sleepyhead. Don't you look appetizing?" he confessed. Within seconds he had his arms around her torso. He pulled her close and nibbled on her earlobe. He felt an erection ascend the instant he touched her. She pushed her pelvis against his, and it drove him wild with desire.

"Mmm! When did you get up?" he heard her moan, but he didn't want to talk. He rubbed his hips against hers as he felt himself growing harder. His appetite for food diminished immediately. He could feel her fingers trailing down his spine to his buttocks. They were interrupted by a knock at the door.

"Shit!" Cole said under his breath as he pulled away from her. Lucy looked at him, confused. "Coming; one moment please," he shouted toward the door.

"I wanted to surprise you. I ordered breakfast," he told her as he walked into the bedroom, looking for a shirt to slip on. He put one on quickly and walked to the door. He blew her a kiss as he reached for the doorknob.

"Gee, I thought *I* was breakfast," Lucy said.

"Hold that thought," Cole replied. Lucy disappeared into the bedroom. He greeted the server, and the server pushed the portable table inside with the food. Cole signed the check as fast as he could, and ushered the waiter out the door. He could smell the fresh coffee as he passed the table, ignored it and went to join Lucy in the bedroom. He stopped at the foot of the bed, then asked with a smirk, "Now, where were we?"

Lucy started to giggle. She motioned for him to join her, watching him drop his shorts and hop in bed. He quickly started cuddling and kissing her softly on her bare breasts.

A half hour later, Cole lay on his back breathless, thinking of his omelet. He chuckled and looked at Lucy.

"What's so funny?" Lucy asked. She snuggled up to his chest and poked him in the side gently.

"I was famished before. Now I don't want to move," he explained and pulled her closer to him.

"I bet the coffee is still hot," Lucy said, and he felt her pull away. She walked in front of him naked and vanished into the next room. He couldn't see her, but heard the clatter of the cups. She came back with two cups of coffee and a piece of pastry.

"Hmm! I like this," Cole said, and raised his eyebrows as she passed him a cup of coffee and a muffin.

"Don't get too used to it, Buddy," she retorted, and wiggled her nose at him. She went around the bed to sit on the other side and slipped in next to him. He raised his cup and took a sip. He took a bite of his muffin, crumbs falling on the sheets.

"I was reading a brochure earlier while waiting for you to wake up. There's a Lobster Festival going on not too far from here. It might be fun. They have a carnival, too. Do you want to go later on?" he asked.

"That sounds like a fun day. Can we pick up breakfast on the way? The omelets were a great idea, but not anymore. They're cold and unappetizing now," she laughed and made a face of disgust.

"Whatever your heart desires. We can grab a bite downstairs at the bistro before we go," Cole suggested.

Lucy nodded. "That sounds perfect," she said between bites of her croissant. It didn't matter where they were or what they did, as long as he was near her. She brought him joy, and that was all he cared about.

***

Rodney arrived in the city of Moncton after dark, a few hours behind Lucy and Cole. He easily found The Delta Beausejour Hotel, since it was located on Main Street. He pulled his hat down low, shielding his face, and drove past the entrance. The parking lot was in the back of the building and marked as a public lot. *Perfect!* he thought. He stopped at the lot gate, pushed the button and grabbed a ticket. He drove to the far end of the lot and parked his truck facing the entrance. He spotted Lucy's truck by her Massachusetts license plate. It was positioned about three lanes to his right. He would be able to see and follow her when she took it out. Rodney turned off the engine and stared up at the windows of the building, wondering what room she might be in. He didn't have much money, so he wouldn't be staying at this hotel. He would find something less expensive.

His eyes felt heavy. Rodney rubbed his face. He was tired, and his arm was throbbing painfully from the dog's bite. He looked around and hunkered down in his seat. He watched all movements for the next hour or so. A couple of cars drove into the lot, parking closer to the entrance. He concluded there was no security guard patrolling the area, so he would be safe to spend his first night in his truck. He slouched down in his seat, zipped his jacket up, crossed his arms in front of him, and closed his eyes.

The sun's morning rays beat down on the front windshield when he woke up. Rodney stretched his arms and opened the driver's window to get some fresh air. He glanced at the dashboard clock, which indicated it was six o'clock. He knew he had time to leave for an hour or so and return with his vehicle before Lucy and Cole would leave the building. They would not leave this early. He started the engine and headed toward Main Street, looking for a place to get coffee and a motel for the next night. He patted his backpack, on the front seat beside him.

The backpack was important to him; it had his disguise. The day before he left, he had purchased dark hair dye, scissors, large dark sunglasses and an oversized hoodie at a pharmacy near Fredericton.

He drove down several of the side streets searching for the right place, until he came across a rundown local motel located on St. Georges street. It was ideal. A neon sign flashed *Vacancy*. He pulled into the lot and parked his truck near the entrance, where he saw another flashing neon sign that indicated the location of the office. The outside of the place needed a fresh coat of paint, and the parking lot area had quite a few potholes. He could see beer cans and take-out boxes overflowing from the garbage bin at the side of the building. He hopped out of his vehicle, swung his backpack over his shoulder, and approached the reception area.

A devilish smile came across his face as he turned the doorknob and entered. This was the ideal place! It had probably been built in the seventies, and never renovated since the day it was built. An older guy with untidy hair was sitting behind the front desk. He seemed unconcerned about anything. His whiskers were pretty long. He needed a shave, but worst of all, he needed a bath more, judging by the sweaty smell of him. His clothes looked like he had been wearing them for the last week, the stains looking as if they had been en-graved into the fabric. He seemed annoyed at being disturbed from "reading" his *Hustler* magazine. He frowned at Rodney as he stepped closer to the front desk. Rodney felt right at home. He dropped his bag on the floor next to the desk and asked, "How much for a room?"

The man looked up at him. He placed his magazine down on the counter, still not moving from his chair, and answered, "Sixty per night, or four hundred per week. If you want maid service, it's extra. Cash only." He closed his eyes and yawned while waiting for Rodney to answer.

"Just the weekend. Three days for now," Rodney replied. He watched the man grab a form and pen from the desk drawer, and shove it in front of him nonchalantly.

"Fill this out," he said, and without getting up, wheeled his chair over to-ward the wall, where the room keys were hanging on a board. He lifted one off its peg and put it on the desk.

"One hundred eighty dollars. You have to pay in advance," he told Rod-ney, as he waited for him to finish filling out the paperwork. Rodney put the pen down and pushed the form away, finished writing all false information on it. He reached down for his backpack, placed it on the top of the desk and unzipped it. Rodney counted out his cash without taking it out of the bag. He re-zipped his bag and gave the cash to the man.

"Room 109, down toward the end of the building to your right," he told Rodney, grabbing the money. The smelly man placed it in a metal box in the top drawer. He ignored Rodney and returned to his magazine.

Rodney picked up the key and his bag, walking out to go find his room. Within minutes he was inside his room. He threw his bag on the bed, then walked to the window and closed the curtains. The room didn't consist of much: a bed with a red faded bedspread, a side table with a lamp, a bureau, and a worn out chair in a corner. He sat on the bed and took out his hair color, scis-sors, and the rest of his disguise. He walked to the bathroom with the scissors and hair color. An hour later, Rodney examined his new self in the mirror. He was quite pleased. He snickered at the image he saw in the mirror and thought, *I wonder if Lucy will like it.* He had cut his hair short and dyed it black. He put on his sunglasses, hat, and hoodie, then looked in the mirror again. He was almost unrecognizable. He was happy with the image he saw in the mirror. Rodney felt powerful enough to defeat anyone, especially that trooper, and win back his sweetheart. He hurried back to his truck to go back to the hotel and wait for his love, Lucy.

Rodney parked in the back lot of the hotel not far from Lucy's SUV, where he had a good view of the vehicle. They would not detect him where he was parked. He had bought two Egg McMuffins and hash browns from a McDonald's drive through on his way back.

He looked at his watch; it was almost noon. *Where the hell are they?* He drummed his fingers on the dashboard while shoving down his meal. He wiped his mouth on his sleeve, and threw the empty bag on the floor of his truck. *Should I go check to make sure they're still inside?* he thought to himself. *But their vehicle is still here. Be patient; you don't want to be spotted.*

Another hour had gone by when he saw them approaching the lot. Cole was holding her hand, laughing. Rodney didn't like the way she was looking at him. Another wave of jealousy passed over him. He narrowed his eyes at Cole. He crouched down lower in his seat until they were seated in the car. He raised his head up to peek, and they were rolling out of the lot. He started the engine and followed them at a safe distance, down Main Street out to the highway. *Wonder where they're going?* They drove for a good fifteen minutes, and took the Shediac exit.

Rodney shadowed them to a small town on the water, where they took a right at an intersection. He noticed the banners hung on telephone poles and the carnival rides in the background. *They're going to a fair. Good place. I can mingle in with the crowd without being seen,* he thought. He took the second entryway into a parking lot across the road. He watched as they stepped out of their vehicle and made their way to the entrance of the festival. Rodney slowly walked in the same direction. He looked around and saw food trucks that sold burgers and cotton candy. There was a large lobster trap on his left selling lobsters, and a tent with performers to his right. Rodney cautiously moved inward, making sure not to be seen by them. There was a crowd of adults and children on the grounds. Rodney could observe them from afar, sometimes turning his back to them or hiding around a corner. Cole stopped at a game and played a few rounds, winning a big stuffed animal for Lucy. Rodney hated the idea that this man won her a stuffed animal. Lucy jumped with excitement and gave Cole a big hug.

. Rodney cringed in disgust when he saw Lucy kiss Cole on the lips. Rodney's hands tightened into fists until his knuckles were white. He wore a look of revulsion as he stood behind the ticket booth, staring at Cole. He loathed that man more with every passing minute.

I have to get rid of him before she becomes too attached to him, Rodney thought. *She belongs to me. She's mine. I'm the one that loves her. I saw her first. How dare he try to take her away from me! She's mine!* Rodney wanted to go up and punch the hell out of him. He wanted to kill the guy so he couldn't touch Lucy anymore. He took a step forward, then realized there were too many witnesses around. He turned and walked back the way he had come, sickened by what he had witnessed. Rodney was so angry! No, furious! He couldn't watch them anymore, so with a hurried pace he passed through the crowd of people in a daze and returned to his vehicle.

He breathed hard through his nose; his lips were pressed firmly together in a thin line by the time he sat in his truck. He gripped the steering wheel and held it firmly. Hatred consumed him. Suddenly he pounded the wheel several times with both fists in frustration. Rodney closed his eyes, trying to gain control of his senses. His whole body was trembling with rage. "I hate you. You will not have her!" he spit between his teeth. He sat immobile in the driver seat for at least a half hour, thinking about how he could annihilate the man with Lucy.

He came up with an answer soon. Rodney started his truck and drove back in the direction of the city. *I have a way to end him*, he thought, and burst into diabolical laughter.

Chapter 10

Lucy and Cole spent a couple of hours at the carnival, laughing and eating junk food. They savored French fries with gravy, candy apples, and corn on the cob. On the way out of the grounds, they decided to explore Main Street. They parked and stepped out of the vehicle, then strolled hand in hand down the street, admiring the quaint stores and restaurants with their outdoor patios. They walked and browsed and looked into the storefront windows until the sun went down.

"Ready to go back?" Cole asked. They sat at one of the outside tables at the Coast Restaurant, where they'd just finished eating nachos and drinking cocktails while watching the traffic go by.

"Yes, I am. I'm a bit tired from all the food and walking," Lucy answered. She leaned over and kissed him lightly on the lips.

"Thanks for a great day. I had so much fun," Lucy said. Cole smiled and pressed his knee against her leg.

"You are welcome; anything to make you happy, Love. Let's get out of here," he told her, and winked. Cole paid the check with his credit card, and they were on their way back to the city for a relaxing evening in their room.

It was a short drive back; they arrived at the hotel within half an hour. On the elevator, Cole placed his hand on her butt to tease her. When they arrived at their room, Cole opened the door, pulled her close to his body and kissed her neck. She playfully pushed back, then something caught her attention.

"AHH! Sweetie, look at *that*!" she squealed and rushed to the bed in the other room. Cole's mouth opened in surprise. *Who sent this?* he thought. He went to sit next to her on the bed. She wrapped her arms around a huge brown teddy bear with a yellow bow. She kept squeezing it against her body.

"It's so soft! Touch it, I love it," she told Cole. She took his hand in hers to feel its fur.

"Who is it from?" he asked her, eyeing the small card attached to the ribbon.

"I don't know; it isn't from you?" she asked teasingly.

Cole shook his head no. He was concerned and suspicious. She frowned at his answer. She pushed the stuffed bear onto the bed, then turned over the card. Cole watched in anticipation. She opened the note, and her eyes widened. She dropped the card and jumped away from the bear as if it had burned her. Her hands went up to her mouth and tears welled up in her eyes. Cole reached down and picked up the card. He clenched his jaw as a feeling of fury passed through him.

The card read, *You belong to me. You're mine.*

Cole took a step toward Lucy. He embraced her tightly as she started to cry softly.

"It's all right. I'm here. He won't hurt you. I won't let anything happen to you. You're safe," he reassured her.

"Who... What does he want? How did he know where we were?" Lucy blurted out questions faster than Cole could answer them. Her sobs echoed in the room. It broke Cole's heart that someone would be so cruel, to do such a thing. *Bastard!* He held Lucy close and escorted her to the living room. They both sat down on the couch.

"I don't know, but if I get a hold of him...," Cole angrily hissed. He knew he couldn't let his emotions get the best of him. Otherwise, it would interfere with his judgment. He needed to focus and protect her.

"Lucy, don't cry. I won't let him hurt you, I promise. I love you. You are my life, always remember that," he tried to reassure her. He was trying to ease her mind and her pain. His hands stroked her back, and he kissed the top of her head. He noticed her body shaking. He gently pushed her from him far enough to wipe her tears away with his hand.

"It's going to be okay. We are going to catch him," he told her confidently. She stopped crying and nodded at him.

"Now, I'm going to go downstairs to inquire as to exactly how this bear got into our room. We might get some kind of description of the guy, a lead maybe. We can catch him if he's around here," Cole said and patted her on the knee. He received a nod and a small smile from her. She snatched his hand and held on to it firmly.

"I'm coming with you. I don't want to stay here alone," she said in a soft tone.

"We are not going to let him ruin our vacation. I'm going to call Troy for backup, to come and join us. He can keep a lookout for anyone suspicious when we're out, and maybe, just maybe, we'll get him. Troy can also get in contact with the police over here, without the son of a bitch knowing we're on to him. It's not a big city, so it should be easier to apprehend him. Okay?" he told her.

Cole walked to the bedroom and dug his cellphone out of his pocket. He snapped a picture of the bear and note, then sent them to Troy. He called Troy as soon as the pictures went through. He took a quick look at Lucy, who was still sitting on the couch rubbing her hands together. She seemed in her own little world, just staring at the floor. On the third ring, Troy answered joyfully, "Hey! How's the happy couple doing?"

"Listen, Troy. I'm wondering if you could take the rest of the weekend off from work, and come and join us in Moncton. The bastard who has been after Lucy is here. He followed us. I need your help. Did you get my pictures?" he asked. He hoped Troy would come to his aid. Otherwise, they were on their own.

"Son of a bitch! You have got to be kidding. What happened?" Troy sound pissed off.

"He just sent Lucy a huge teddy bear with a note that says, 'You belong to me,'" Cole explained, as he paced the floor of the bedroom. His voice was quiet, not wanting to upset Lucy any more than she was.

"We need a plan to catch him. Think about it, and I'll be there as soon as I can. I'll call you when I get there," Troy told him. Cole felt better knowing that he wouldn't be alone with Lucy. He put his phone away and went to the living room.

"How are you doing? Troy is on his way here to help. We are going to go downstairs to the front desk. You are to stay close to me, okay?" he instructed. Cole placed her delicate hand in his and squeezed it slightly. "It's going to be all right. Let's go."

Within minutes they were standing at the front desk, facing a young lady named Debra. Cole put his hand on the counter and waited for her to finish whatever she was doing on her computer. He shifted his weight from one foot to the other impatiently; every minute counted now, if they were to catch him. Finally, she spoke. "Good evening, how may I assist you?" She looked up at him and smiled.

"Hi, I'm in room 803. A large teddy bear was delivered to our room earlier today. I was wondering what you could tell me about it. Who brought it in? There was no name on the card," Cole inquired, keeping his eye on his surroundings. He was no longer the boyfriend; he was in cop mode now.

"Yes, I remember the young man coming by with it. He asked to have the bear to be dropped off to your room. Is something wrong?" she asked with concern.

"I'm a state trooper from the US, vacationing here. I believe the man who delivered that bear followed us here. He is wanted in Maine," he told her. He took out his badge and discreetly showed it to her, then put it away. He reached over and placed his hand on Lucy's lower back to reassure her.

"Did he ask for our room number, or ask for us by name?" Cole questioned her. Debra didn't respond right away; she seemed to be thinking about it.

"He asked to have it dropped off to Lucy Marvin's room, but he did not have the room number. We would not give him your room number," she answered.

"Could you describe him to me? What he was wearing?" Cole inquired, hoping she would remember the guy.

"Do you want to speak to our security manager? He should have a video of him from the front desk camera," she informed them.

Cole nodded at her. "Yes, that's perfect! I appreciate it." He watched as Debra called security. Cole waited patiently, tapping his foot on the floor. *Maybe we'll be lucky and have a picture of the bastard on video*, he thought.

"He'll be right over, if you'll have a seat. He shouldn't be long," she said, and pointed at two chairs in the lobby.

"Thank you," Cole said, then escorted Lucy over to the seats.

"Hopefully they caught him on camera," he said, but Lucy didn't say a word. She just nodded quietly. Lucy's eyes darted from one person to another in the lobby. Cole noticed a man approaching the front desk in a dark blue suit. He spoke to the girl at the front desk, then turned and started walking toward their direction. Cole stood up to greet him.

"Hi, I'm Robert Wood, head of security. How may I be of service?" he said and shook Cole's hand firmly.

"Nice to meet you. My name is Cole Baker. I'm a Maine State Trooper, and this is my girlfriend Lucy Marvin," Cole said. Lucy didn't shake his hand or move from her chair. She just nodded at him.

"I hear you are having a problem; how may I help?" he asked again, and sat down next to them.

"I'll explain briefly what is going on. Lucy has someone who has been stalking her for some time. She just received a stuffed bear with this note," he said. Cole handed Robert the card, and watched as he read it. Robert he gave it back to Cole quickly.

"You think he followed you here? Wow!" Robert exclaimed. "Let's go see if we caught him on the security footage. Follow me." Robert led them down a small hallway to an office that had several monitors; some surveyed the lobby, others the front and back entrances. Two security guards were sitting at a desk observing the cameras.

"Michel, could you find the film for the front desk for earlier today?" Robert asked. Cole and Lucy waited patiently without saying a word as he searched. Robert sat down at the monitor to start reviewing the tape.

"There," Cole pointed at the screen. No one spoke as they viewed the screen. A man with sunglasses and a black hoodie moved to the front desk. His head was bowed low, obviously avoiding the camera; the brim of his hat was hiding his face, and he was holding the huge bear under his arm. He briefly spoke to the lady at the desk, gave her the bear, then left the same way he had entered.

"Do you recognize him?" Robert asked Cole who was standing next to his chair, leaning forward for a better look.

Cole shook his head and said, "No." He turned to Lucy next to him to see if she knew him. "Lucy?" She just shook her head no.

"Well, he concealed his face. But he isn't a big guy: average weight and height. Let's go talk to Debra at the front desk. Maybe she can tell us a little more about him," Robert suggested to them and led the way.

Cole took Lucy's hand in his and followed Robert closely. Cole was disappointed they didn't put a face to the bastard with the security footage. They returned to the lobby to talk to the girl, but all she could add was that he had black hair, and had only asked to have the bear delivered to their room. Robert told them he would alert hotel security about the man, and if he resurfaced they would apprehend him. He suggested they report the incident to the Royal Canadian Mounted Police of the area, but Cole declined. He would take care of it. Cole thanked Robert, then he and Lucy returned to their room; he was dissatisfied with the outcome.

***

Lucy was in a state of shock. Her mind was a whirlwind of questions. How did he know where she was? Who was this man? What did he want? She walked into her hotel room and collapsed on the couch. She had seen the video, but didn't know this guy. Cole sat beside her and pulled her to his side. Tears filled her eyes once again. No one spoke for a minute.

"Don't worry. I won't let him harm you. I'm here for you. He isn't going to ruin our weekend. Troy will be here to help me catch him, and we'll find another hotel so he can't find us," Cole assured her. He rubbed her back softly.

"What does he *want?*" Lucy asked in a shaky voice, tears falling down her cheeks. She covered her face with her hands and sobbed.

"I don't know. It's going to be all right. Now, wipe those tears away. Why don't you take a shower? Then we'll go out to dinner. By the time we get back, maybe Troy will be here," he said, trying to cheer her up.

"I don't feel like going out," she answered. She looked toward the bedroom and saw the bear once again. "And could you get rid of that bear?" she asked. A cold chill ran down her back. It was really creepy to think that someone was stalking her. She watched as Cole got up, marched to the bedroom and gripped the stuffed animal by the head. He opened the door and threw it out into the hallway.

"Why don't I run you a hot bath, and we can order room service? We can snuggle in bed and watch a movie, and..." Cole suggested.

"Sure, that sounds nice," Lucy whispered, still feeling unsure. Cole offered his hand to help her up from her seat and led her to the bathroom. She didn't resist; she just obeyed, in a daze. Cole reached down and turned on the hot water. He grabbed a bottle of bubble bath from the counter, twisted the top off, and poured a little into the water.

"Do you need any help taking your clothes off? I'm able and willing to help," he said with a smirk. He took one step forward and was next to her. His fingers unbuttoned the top button of her shirt, then the next button. It brought a smile to her face. She slapped his hand and giggled at him. He pulled back, smiling.

"Well, excuse me!" he said and raised his hands up in the air. She forgot everything but him for a moment..

"I can do it. Thank you so much for everything, babe," she told him, snickering. His hand came down around her waist and started tickling her. She squirmed and wiggled around the bathroom. He knew how to make her feel better. They were both laughing loudly while hugging each other in seconds.

Lucy sat in the tub, her legs up against the wall, relaxing as the hot water enveloped her body and took away her worries. She closed her eyes and thought, *I hope this relationship works out. He's so good to me. I'm falling in love with him. Love! Yes, I love him, but will he break my heart like my husband did? Stop it, Lucy!* She was distracted when she heard Cole speaking to someone. It must be Troy. She was happy Troy was coming to help catch the son of a bitch. She stepped out of the tub and dried off. The bath had relaxed her, so she decided to get into bed to rest. She pulled the comforter over her body. Lucy felt warm under the blanket, and secure. Cole came in and sat next to her on the edge of the bed.

"Feeling better? You sure smell good!" he said. He inhaled her scent, then leaned forward and gently brushed a few strands of wet hair off her face. He kissed her on the cheek.

"Yes. I heard you talking to someone on the phone. Was it Troy?" she asked, touching his arm lightly. He nodded.

"He's coming to join us. He'll be here later on tonight. I hope you don't mind," Cole replied, his eyes focused on hers.

"Not at all; that's great. I'm going to go to bed early. I'm not really hungry. I kind of lost my appetite, and I'm exhausted," she told him. Cole stood up.

"No worries. I'm just going to wait up for Troy. I won't be up too late," he said. He kissed her on the lips, then pulled back a few inches and said, "I love you."

"I love you, too," she replied without thinking. It was true.

"I'll be right here in the living room. I know you're tired, so don't worry, sleep. I'll come to bed later," he reassured her by patting her on the knee. She nodded and closed her eyes. Cole sauntered to the door of the bedroom. He turned around for one last peek at her before he quietly shut the door behind him.

***

Rodney lay on the bed at his dingy motel room. He was staring at the paint chipping off the ceiling. His hands were behind his head and his ankles were crossed. He wondered if Lucy had liked his gift. It was a lot better than what her boyfriend had won for her at the fair. He ground his teeth; how he hated the way the trooper put his arms around her waist and kissed her! *I saw her first, and how dare he think that he can take her away from me?!* Rodney formed two tight fists, then punched the mattress and kicked the bed with his feet several times at the thought of him touching her. *I have to get rid of him; that's it.* He sat up, resting his head against the headboard. *How? How can I get rid of him? A knife?* Rodney didn't have any weapons, and Cole was a cop. Rodney was not a very good fighter, especially hand to hand. Cole would disarm him, and he might lose the battle. It was not a good idea to take the cop on armed with a knife.

He tapped his finger against his mouth, thinking. There was one thing he was awesome at, and he had experience with it. He knew how to handle this weapon. Yes, that was it. He didn't have to be too close, and Lucy would never know it came from him. Cole would never see it coming. Rodney started to laugh uncontrollably, so much that he had cramps in his belly. He placed a hand on his stomach. He would put his plan together tomorrow. Right now, he needed sleep. He reached over to the night table, shut off the light, and closed his eyes. Within minutes, he was fast asleep.

The next morning, Rodney woke up a new man. He had a plan. He stretched his arms up high, trying to wake up. He had slept fully dressed. Rodney was on a mission. He sat up at the edge of the bed, slipped on his boots and immediately left his motel room. He drove down the streets of Moncton looking for a specific store. An hour passed, and he was about to give up when he took a right down Mapleton Avenue. Suddenly, he beamed from ear to ear. He had found the right store. He turned the wheel into the parking lot of Cabela's, a hunting and fishing store. He hopped out of his truck and hurried to the front door of the store. He entered and strolled around looking at camouflage outfits. He saw what he was looking for on the far wall. Rodney smirked and admired the selection. He needed one that was simple to use and effective at a good distance. He was familiar with this weapon; he'd been using one since he was a young boy, for hunting and target shooting. It was the only passion he'd ever had, except for Lucy. What a selection! Hanging on the wall in front of him was a wide variety of bows and arrows. He was carefully examining the variety when a salesperson interrupted his focus.

"Good morning! Can I help you with anything?" he asked. Rodney didn't take his eyes of the weapons, studying them intently.

"Yes, I'm looking for a hunting bow," Rodney said, without looking at the salesman. He wanted to laugh when he thought what he wanted it for.

"Could I see the Warden 62 recurve bow?" he asked, and pointed at the weapon as excitement invaded him. Rodney's heart was pounding fast against his chest. He avidly watched the salesman take down the bow; he handed it to Rodney.

"So, it's one of the best quality bows we have. What do you think?" he asked Rodney. Rodney held it in his right hand, feeling the weight. He traced the arch with the tip of his fingers. He was in his own world as he examined the weapon. He approved of the curved wooden handle that fit his grip perfectly, and the fiberglass limbs. He loved it, and the price was in range. He handed it back to the salesman who placed it on top of the countertop. Rodney nodded.

"What do you think? Do you need any arrows?" the salesperson asked.

"Yes, I would like six carbon steel arrow shafts with six Montec three-blade broadheads, if you have them. Oh, and I would prefer a case to the cardboard box," Rodney said confidently. He pointed to a soft canvas case nearby.

"No problem. Anything else?" the salesman asked. Rodney shook his head. He paid cash for his purchases without saying another word, and walked out of the store. His heart was thumping hard from excitement. *I am ready! I'll drive to my usual hiding spot in the parking lot, and wait for the right moment. I'll take him out. He will not stand in my way of getting my true love.*

Chapter 11

Cole was happy Lucy was resting. He knew she'd been through a lot the last few hours. Just the fact that she had a madman tracking her every move without knowing what he really wanted from her was nerve-wracking. Cole sat on the couch and put his feet on the coffee table. He picked up the remote control and turned on the TV, but his mind wasn't on whatever sports event was on the tube. He checked his watch. Troy should arrive any minute. Cole waited patiently.

A hour had passed when Cole heard a soft knock on the door. He hurried over and swung it open. Troy was standing in the hall, with a backpack over his left shoulder.

"Hi, how are you doing?" Troy asked. He marched into the room and dropped his bag by the couch, then sat down in the chair facing it.

"Good. Lucy is sleeping. I've been waiting for you. Do you want a beer?" Cole asked. Cole didn't wait for Troy to answer, he just handed him a beer from the mini bar.

"So, tell me what's going on." Troy said. He took a sip of his beer and slouched down in his chair. Cole flopped down on the couch before answering.

"The bastard followed us here. He sent Lucy a large stuffed animal that was delivered to our room. He had the balls to write 'You belong to me. You're mine.' on the card. Lucy freaked out; she's really frightened. I felt so bad for her. So, you and I have to hatch a plan. Maybe we can catch him before we return home. He doesn't know you're here," Cole explained. Troy listened attentively.

"Have you reported it to the police yet?" Troy asked. He glanced at the television then back at Cole.

"Not yet. I was thinking about doing it tomorrow. The problem is, what can they do? Nothing much; they'll just file a report. I was thinking when we go out tomorrow, you'll hang back to observe and see if someone follows us. What do you think?" Cole finished his beer and placed the bottle on the coffee table while waiting for an answer.

"I can do that. Where did you plan on going tomorrow? It'll have to be a public place, somewhere he feels comfortable and thinks he could get away, not strolling down Main Street," Troy said.

Cole picked up the tourist brochures that were spread out on the table next to him. He leafed through them for a moment, then decided on one. "How about if we go to lunch and I take her golfing tomorrow? Here, at Fox Creek Golf Club," Cole suggested, passing the country club pamphlet to Troy.

Troy looked at it then nodded. "Yes, this might work. It has a map of the area, and I can tee off behind you and follow you discreetly. If I see anyone suspicious around. I can keep an eye out for him," Troy answered, handing the brochure back.

"All right then, we're all set. Where is your room?" Cole asked as he got up to retrieve another beer from the fridge.

"I'm right across the hall from you. Thanks for the beer. I'm beat, so I'll see you in the morning, around ten; that sounds good." Troy said. He stood up, picked up his bag from the floor, and walked to the door wearily. Cole followed him.

"Okay, I'll see you tomorrow. Hopefully we'll get that bastard," Cole told him. Cole slapped Troy lightly on the back as he exited. Troy took his key out of his pocket and opened his door across the hall

"Thanks, man," Cole said. His best friend nodded and disappeared behind his door.

***

Rodney rose early and picked up an egg sandwich and coffee from one of the drive-thru restaurants. He sat in his truck watching for Lucy and the cop with his bow and arrow on the seat beside him. He was ready to eliminate the threat. Rodney gobbled the last bite of his meal and shoved the paper wrapper in the empty bag, then threw it on the floor. His eyes were locked on the entrance of the parking lot; he waiting patiently for her appearance. Rodney turned his head toward his newly acquired weapon and touched it gently. A sensation of power washed over him. He was now closer to having Lucy for himself, to love. Once he got rid of that big trooper, she would be his forever.

Rodney's attention was alerted when he noticed three people walking toward the lot. *There she is! She is so beautiful, in her blue jeans and pink top.* He pursed his lips and narrowed his eyes at the trooper. He was holding Lucy's hand, and talking to the other man. Rodney knew the extra man was Cole's friend, another state trooper from Maine. Rodney had seen him patrolling around Houlton. *Why is he here? That's odd. Maybe they know about me!*

Rodney decided he would have to be very cautious today so he wouldn't be spotted. He didn't want to get apprehended. He watched the third man with narrowed eyes. The newcomer didn't hop into Lucy's truck with them. Rodney crouched down low in his seat. Only the top of his head showed above the dashboard. The second man got into a gray truck, but he didn't leave; he seemed to be waiting for something. Rodney saw Lucy's SUV depart the lot, but he couldn't take the chance of trailing them. *You have to find out if he knows about you,* he thought.

He sat up when Lucy's truck disappeared around the building. He started his truck and continued out of the parking lot. His eyes were glued to his rearview mirror, his hands sweating from the thrill of the hunt, wondering if that other man would follow him. Lucy's truck went right on Main Street, so he did the same. Rodney continued down Main Street, heading toward a shopping area. He stopped at an intersection when the light turned red. He scanned the area behind him; the gray truck was still there. He reached over and picked up his hat, then pulled it down low on his forehead. The light changed to green; Rodney went forward, checking his mirrors and keeping his speed steady. The man was still there, behind another car. Rodney could see Lucy's truck up ahead.

Should I proceed, or turn back? Rodney slowed down, all the while keeping his eyes on Lucy's truck and the man trailing him. He kept going straight ahead down the street, now entering another town called Dieppe. The traffic was steady. Rodney bit the inside of his mouth, tapping his fingers on steering wheel nervously while trying to decide if he should continue or turn into a side street. Sweat beads dripped down his face. He wiped his brow with the back of his hand. He watched as Lucy's vehicle turned right down an avenue. Rodney continued to the next street and turned left. This road was taking him to a highway. He peered into his mirrors. The second trooper was still tracking him from afar.

Why didn't he turn right when Lucy did? Rodney couldn't take any chances, so he turned onto the highway and sped up. The gray truck stopped following him, and was nowhere in sight. He had stopped tailing Rodney.

Rodney signed with relief as he rolled down the highway. Lucy's boyfriend and that other man were trying to corner him, but he was too smart for them. He put the radio on and laughed loudly.

***

Troy sat in his vehicle waiting for Cole and Lucy to leave the parking lot to go to lunch at the country club. It wasn't long before he saw a red pickup truck exit the parking lot of the hotel, just a minute after Cole and Lucy. His instinct told him he had a lead. It was as if the driver was biding his time until they came out. *Is it a coincidence? With Maine license plates?* Within a minute, the red vehicle was going the same direction as Lucy and Cole. Troy dropped a few car lengths back for a while, not wanting to scare him away or alert him he was being followed. *What if this is the wrong guy?* By the time he entered the town of Dieppe, he had reached over and opened the dash. He pushed papers around until he found a pen and paper. He laid the paper on the seat and wrote down the license plate: H6G 769. The license plate was from Maine. He had a good feeling about this, so he turned left toward the highway. It was the opposite of the route Cole and Lucy were taking. Troy turned the same way, still not convinced he was wrong—but the truck took off down the highway. Troy pulled to the side of the road and watched the vehicle disappear down the freeway.

The first thing he wanted to do was inform Cole. He decided to go find them instead of calling Cole on his cellphone. He made a U-turn in the road as soon as the coast was clear. He crossed the intersection and continued down the road until he spotted Fox Creek Golf Club. Troy parked his truck and hurried inside. Almost running, he went up the stairs and into the restaurant entrance.

"Good morning, may I help you?" A young lady dressed all in black greeted him at the entryway of the bistro. He glanced at her quickly, then scanned the dining area.

"No, I'm all set. I see my friends, thank you," Troy told her, and walked toward Cole's and Lucy's table. They were sill looking at the breakfast menu and sipping their coffee. He pulled a chair back and sat down. Cole put his menu down, and Lucy peeked over the top of hers.

"Well, what did you find? Did someone follow us?" Cole asked right away. He took a sip of his coffee, waiting for an answer. Troy gave him the piece of paper.

Cole took it and glanced at it. "A license plate number?" he asked, a little confused. He handed the paper back to Troy.

"It belongs to a red pickup truck. He immediately shadowed you guys when you left the hotel parking lot, so I tracked him. But he turned onto the highway at the intersection up the street. I think he knew I was following him, and he got spooked. Anyway..." Troy was interrupted by the waitress holding a pot of coffee in one hand and a menu in the other. She placed the menu on the table in front of him.

"Good morning. Coffee?" she asked. He looked up at her, smiled and nodded. Troy didn't speak, he just waited patiently until she was done. When she finished pouring his coffee, he said. "Thank you."

"I'll be back in a few minutes to take your order," she said, and left them alone to continue their conversation.

"The license plate of this truck is from Maine. What are the chances someone from Maine would be here following you?" Troy asked, and raised his hand to high-five Cole. He gently slapped his hand.

"We have to investigate this lead," Troy said. He noticed Lucy's eyes had widened, but she never said a word.

"Shit! That's great. We might have caught a break. Good job. When we return tomorrow, we'll check it out," Cole said and smiled at his friend. He had been concerned about informing Cole of what he had found. A few golfers were putting on one of the greens about a hundred yards down a hillside; Troy looked around, now that he'd passed on the information, and saw the green scenery with beautiful flowers, pruned shrubs, and large emerald trees.

Troy reached for the cream in the middle of the table. He felt a hand on his forearm. He looked up and saw Lucy's eyes tear up, and her lower lip trembled a little bit. "Thank you so much," was all she said, in a low voice. He covered her hand with his and squeezed it lightly then nodded at her.

"Anything for you, Lucy. Now, I'm famished! What looks good?" he asked, and picked up the menu.

***

Lucy felt as if a load had been lifted off her shoulders. She was confident the boys would catch this guy, now that they had a lead. She wasn't comfortable waiting until tomorrow to identify this man. She was staring at the golfers on the green. She was debating in her head if they should cut short their weekend and return home immediately. This bastard was here, in this country; Cole and Troy had no jurisdiction to apprehend and arrest him. At least in Maine, they would have the backing of the police force to rely on. Lucy was quiet, not listening to the guys' conversation, lost in thought. She felt a hand on her knee; it was Cole's of course. She turned her head to look at him.

"Are you okay? You're so quiet," he asked. She noticed Troy was also watching her.

"I'm fine. I was just thinking, maybe we should cut our weekend short and return home, so you can further inquire into this lead. I'm nervous that he is so close. You and Troy don't have back up here. You know what I mean," she said. She was hoping he would agree. She tilted her head at him waiting for his response.

"I understand. Are you sure that's what you want?" Cole asked.

Troy cut in and said, "You know, she's right. We would be in a better position to catch him if we were home, and we would have the cooperation of the force. Here, we're foreigners, and they don't see this situation as we do."

"I agree with Troy," she told Cole. Cole nodded at his friend.

Cole placed his napkin on the table and pushed his chair back. "Very well then; let's get the hell out of here. We have an asshole to catch," he told them.

Lucy's gave him another smile. She took his hand in hers. "Let's go home," she said, elated they were going back.

An hour later they had packed, checked out of the hotel, and were on the highway going back to her house. They figured they would be back in Maine within four hours. Lucy was sitting in the passenger seat, letting Cole take the wheel. She was listening to the music on the radio, drumming her fingers on her knee as her head bobbed up and down. All her worries had been put aside. They were going to catch this stalker now that they had a clue.

She heard Cole's laughter invade the car.

"What's so funny?" she asked, starting to giggle with him. She loved the way he made her feel so comfortable, like she was the only one who mattered.

"I wish I had a video of you right now, grooving to the music," he told her. He kept one eye on the road, and winked at her with the other. She slapped his arm lovingly.

"Oh, yeah! I'll let you film me naked when you imprison that asshole. How's that for an incentive?" she told him. They both cracked up into laughter once again.

"I'll hold you to that," he replied with a chuckle.

Chapter 12

Rodney drove down to the first exit off the highway and turned back toward Moncton. He went straight to the motel and parked right in front of his door. He slammed the door of his vehicle and ran inside. *I have to leave before that cop finds me! I have to hurry!* he kept thinking. Rodney quickly picked up his belongings and stuffed them in the duffel bag. He had barely escaped being caught.

He knew Cole had reinforcements now, in trying to keep him away from Lucy, but it wouldn't deter him from getting to his Lucy. Within five minutes, Rodney was on his way back home to Maine, where he felt he had a better chance to be with Lucy again. He knew Lucy was only away for the weekend, so he could wait one day. The town and the woods around her house had been his sanctuary, where he could dream without intrusion. He would have to get rid of the obstacles that prevented him from being with her. She loved him, too. Rodney was sure of it.

Soon, he was in line at the US border to re-enter the country. As he approached the border, he became increasingly nervous. A feeling of dread passed through him. Rodney squirmed in his seat and started biting his thumbnail. His passport was beside him on the console. He looked at his passenger seat and wasn't sure if he was allowed to bring in the bow and arrow he had bought. *It is what it is! What's the worst that can happen?* he thought. *The officer will just confiscate it.* Another car pulled out, and he was next. Rodney inhaled deeply, and exhaled slowly. He barely pressed on the gas pedal and the truck moved forward. He stopped at the booth. The border officer stepped out, extending his hand for Rodney's identification while examining something on his computer. He looked at the passport and then at Rodney.

"Hi, Rodney. I almost didn't recognize you. You changed your hair color. What, are you trying to catch a girl?" he joked with a smirk. Rodney remembered this guy. He was a customer Rodney had served many times at the garage. He also knew the guy lived in Houlton. A sense of relief passed through him. Rodney raked his fingers through his hair.

"Yeah, you like it? I thought I'd try something new," Rodney said, as casually as he could. His insides were shaking, he was so nervous.

"What were you doing in Canada?" the officer asked, passing Rodney's passport back to him. He placed it on the passenger seat next to the case that contained his bow and arrows.

"I just went to visit an old friend of my grandmother's who needed help moving," he lied nervously.

"Where abouts in Canada did you go?" the officer asked, peering in the back of Rodney's truck.

"I was in Moncton for the weekend. Nice city!" Rodney answered.

"Okay, I'll see you around—and keep out of trouble," the border officer joked. Rodney nodded at him and rolled slowly away. Rodney laughed sarcastically. He drove back into town while making plans on how and when he would eliminate his obstacle, Cole.

***

A few hours later, Cole and Lucy were cruising down the highway, approaching the border. Cole glanced over and admired his love sleeping. Her head rested on the headrest. He reached over and stroked her thigh tenderly.

"Wake up, Hon, we're almost home," Cole said. Lucy had dozed off during the ride back to the US, about an hour ago. She slowly opened her eyes and turned her head toward him with a smile. *How beautiful she is when she wakes up,* he thought. Cole never wanted to leave her side, never again. She leaned over to put her hand on the inside of his thigh and stroked upward. Lucy kissed his cheek, then her wet mouth moved to his earlobe while he drove into the border crossing area. Her tongue sent a shiver down his spine.

"You better stop that, otherwise we might get arrested at the border," he jested with her. He could see the administration building up ahead. Lucy pulled away and sat up straight, but kept her hand on his leg. He drove up to the border booth and stopped. The officer looked up; Cole knew Jim from working with him several times over the years, concerning the border patrol.

"Well, this must be my lucky day. How are you, Cole?" Jim asked. Cole handed him their passports.

"Good afternoon, Jim. I'm fine; how about you? This is my girlfriend Lucy," Cole said. Jim leaned toward the window.

"Same old, same old. Nice to meet you, Lucy," Jim answered. The officer took a step back and entered the booth. Cole watched him open and briefly examine their passports. Jim then came back out to stand at the driver's door, handing the passports back to Cole.

"Must be my lucky day for people from Houlton," Jim said. Something clicked in Cole's mind. *Someone else came through?* he thought. *It must be him: the stalker.*

"Who came by, Jim?" Cole asked quickly, trying to get information.

"Rodney: you know, the guy who works at the gas station in town. Funny thing was, he'd dyed his hair black. I almost didn't recognize him," Jim said with a grin.

"What was *he* doing in Canada?" Cole asked, intrigued. *Why he was there, and why did he color his hair? Could he be the one? No. There's no way...*

"He said he went to help someone move," Jim answered. "What's the sudden interest?" he asked seriously.

"Let me ask you another question. He wouldn't have been driving a red truck, would he?" Cole questioned. His heart started to beat faster. He glanced at Lucy. She was listening attentively to every word. She raised her hand to cover her mouth, her eyes widening in surprise.

"Yes, how did you know? You're all set," Jim replied, looking down at the long line behind them. He tapped the door frame of the truck. Cole moved forward in disbelief. He couldn't believe Rodney was the one. He didn't seem the type, but Cole had learned during his years on the force that you just never know.

"Cole, whatever you are thinking about Rodney, it's not possible. He's just a shy, innocent kid. He wouldn't hurt a fly. God, he barely talks to me. He hardly knows me," Lucy said.

"I don't know, but I'm going to check it out anyway. Too many coincidences," Cole answered. Rage invaded his being. He could barely think. *That fucking bastard! How could he put Lucy through all that?* He squeezed the wheel tighter, unable to focus on anything but Rodney. *Of all people, how could it be him? Why?*

"Oh! Come on, Cole. You're barking up the wrong tree. Rodney is not capable of all those things," Lucy insisted.

"I'm still going to check it out," Cole insisted. He saw the disappointment in Lucy's eyes. He also saw a disapproving frown on her face. Lucy turned her head toward the window. She wouldn't look at him. He reached out to touch her knee, but she pushed it away. Cole felt pain in his heart. He didn't want to fight with her. He just wanted to keep her safe. It was clear that she wasn't convinced Rodney could be her stalker. She didn't utter another word all the way to his house. She was mad at him, and Cole felt sad, but he needed to protect her.

Cole pulled into his driveway and shut off the engine. He watched her as she opened the passenger door and walked around the car. She swung his door wide and stood still with her hand on the door handle. Cole stepped out and went to stand inches from her. Lucy's hair was blowing in the wind, and her eyes were cast downwards. *She's not going to look at me, is she? She's angry with me. Our first weekend together and we come home, and she's upset. Great, just great,* he thought.

"Lucy, don't leave; stay with me tonight. I don't want to fight with you. I'll tell you what. I'll have Troy check out Rodney. I don't want you to go home alone," he pleaded with her. He raised his hand to push the hair away from her face. She jerked her head away from his touch. Cole closed his eyes and sighed heavily.

"Okay, I'll be here if you need me or you want to talk. I had a fabulous time. I'll call you later," he told her. Not a word came out of her mouth. She still avoided his gaze, and her lower lip was trembling a little. Cole didn't want her to cry. It broke his heart to see her hurting. *For what? For Rodney?* He moved to the side and grabbed his bag from the back seat. He swung his bag over his shoulder and walked up the porch steps. *I'll let her cool down and go see her in a few hours, after I get more information about Rodney and the red truck,* he thought. He watched as she got into the car and drove away.

***

Lucy felt a tear escape and roll down her cheek while driving away from Cole's house. *Turn the car around and go tell him you're sorry. He might be right about Rodney. Go back, hold him in your arms; you love this man. Don't throw this relationship away because of a stupid argument about a boy,* she thought. *I shouldn't be mad at him, but I cannot believe Rodney, that shy kid, would want to harm me in any way.*

She felt stressed. She rubbed her neck, which hurt from sleeping upright. *Just go home, take a long hot bath and rethink this whole mess,* she thought. *I'll call Cole later when I feel better.* She parked the car, got her bag out of the trunk, and went up the porch steps. Her keys were in her hand, ready unlock her front door. She didn't notice another large bouquet of wildflowers on her rocking chair. Lucy's hands began to shake so badly she was having a hard time fitting the key into the keyhole. *What if Cole's right? What if Rodney would hurt me?* Finally, she managed to open the door and re-locked it the instant she was inside. She dropped her bag on the floor. Lucy could barely breathe. Her eyes were darting from right to left as she listened for anything abnormal; she was paralyzed with fear. *What if he's here somewhere? But where would he be? You are imagining things, Lucy. Stop it!*

She dug her hand in her back pocket and removed her phone. She immediately called Cole. Her phone glued to her ear, Lucy heard the first ring, then a second. *Please answer, Cole. Please.*

"Hello," Cole finally answered.

"Cole, I'm sorry. You're right, but I don't know what to do. I'm sorry," she sobbed quietly. Her back against the front door, she was unable to move any further inside the house. How stupid she had been, letting this small argument divide them.

"I'll come by in a little while. Get settled in, take a bath. I'll be there soon. It's going to be okay," he said. She agreed, and the phone went dead.

***

Rodney had spent a whole hour harvesting the perfect flowers when he arrived back in town. He promptly took them to the bungalow and left them on the chair for Lucy. One by one he had smelled each flower before placing it into the bouquet. He added a yellow ribbon this time instead of pink, which he had found in his grandmother's sewing kit. He stood back to admire the masterpiece he was giving her. He went back to the woods to hide and wait patiently. This time, he wasn't sitting on the ground. He climbed up high in one of the large trees. Rodney inched up the tree one branch at a time, being careful to make sure every branch could support his weight. A backpack was on his back, and his bow and arrow were strapped across his chest. He settled in to wait for her. He wasn't going to make the mistake of being on the ground again, not after what happened with the dog. The weekend was over, so she should be home this evening. He was patient and comfortable in the tree, so he could wait.

Rodney loved the woods. He loved the smell of the earth, and how the animals scurried away when he came near them. It was where he spent most of his free time, exploring and discovering new things. His thoughts went back when he was a boy, and his grandfather showed him how to use a bow until he had perfected it. Grandpa had made him targets in the woods to find and shoot down. Rodney and his grandfather used to go deer hunting in this forest. He sat on the thick, sturdy branch eating a granola bar, hanging out and watching. He tilted his head and smirked when he saw Lucy's car coming up the driveway. He observed her every move closely until she closed the door behind her. *Didn't she see my flowers?* She hadn't taken them inside; she hadn't even gone toward them. She'd liked his other flowers. Rodney felt a bit sad. She would take them in and wear them in her hair when she saw them; he was sure of it. "Anything to make you happy," he whispered. He rested his back against the trunk and made himself comfortable.

***

As soon as Lucy drove away, Cole got in his truck and drove to the police station as fast as he could. He ran up the stairs, taking them two at a time, barging through one door after another. Cole pulled out a chair and sat down at his precinct desk. He furiously typed the license plate number into the Department of Motor Vehicles program that Troy had given him. Cole drummed his fingers impatiently while waiting to get confirmation it belonged to Rodney. His eyes widened when the answer popped up. It wasn't Rodney name, but his grandfather's on the truck's registration. Cole's jaw tightened and his nostrils flared as a wave of anger rushed through his body. He had the bastard! *That's* why he never knew Rodney had a truck. Now that he had identified the vehicle, he needed to find Rodney. He technically couldn't arrest him, because he needed proof. Rodney hadn't done anything illegal by sending her gifts or following her, but Cole was going put the fear of God into him and try to keep him away from Lucy. He didn't even have verification Rodney was the one who had hurt King, or was the one who was watching Lucy. The best Cole could do was bring him in and interrogate him.

Cole decided to go find Rodney—but first, he needed backup. He grabbed his phone and called Troy.

"Hi, Troy. Could you meet me at Ted's Garage? I know who we're looking for. I know the truck. I'm going to go talk to this asshole," Cole said.

"Wow! How? Who?" Troy asked.

"I'll explain when you get there," Cole said.

"I'll meet you there in five minutes," Troy replied.

Cole left the building and drove the short distance to the garage. He scanned the parking lot, looking for Rodney without success. He saw Troy pulling up next to him. When Troy jumped out of the car, Cole did the same.

"Ready? Let's go," Cole said. Cole explained the conversation that he had with the border control officer, Jim. Troy listened closely as they walked into the open garage bay. Cole's eyes searched for Rodney, but he was nowhere to be seen.

"Good afternoon, guys. What can I do for you?" Bob, the mechanic on duty, asked. He wiped his hands on a blue cloth while walking toward them. He knew them both.

"Hi Bob. Is Rodney around?" Cole asked, as he scrutinized every corner of the place. Cole's fists were balled up tight; he was ready for Rodney.

"Sorry, he's not here. He took a few days off, I was told. Why?" Bob asked.

"We just wanted to talk to him. Nothing important," Troy replied quickly. Cole didn't want to give Bob any information that might be relayed back to Rodney. Cole smiled and nodded at Bob.

"Do you know when he's supposed to return? I wanted to know if he would be available to wash my truck," Cole said casually.

"He's expected back at work tomorrow. I'll let him know," Bob offered.

"Don't bother, I'll stop by again tomorrow. Thanks a lot, Bob," Cole said. He and Troy walked back to their vehicles.

"What now? How about we go to his house? He might be there," Troy said, reaching for the handle of his car door.

"Leave your car here. Hop in with me, and let's go check it out," Cole said. Troy got into Cole's passenger seat.

"Cole, I know you're mad and want to give this guy a beating, but we have to do it by the book. Otherwise, nothing will stick. You know that. I don't want you to get into trouble," Troy said. He buckled his seatbelt and looked at Cole, waiting for an answer. Cole just nodded, too furious to speak. *If I get my hands on that son of a bitch*, he thought.

"Cole, did you hear me?" Troy asked.

"Yes, I understand," Cole said. His eyes were narrowed, locked on the road, and his jaw clenched. They drove down one street for a few miles, then turned right on a narrow dirt road. Cole could see the old battered farmhouse and a barn up ahead. He steered his truck up the driveway and stopped near the porch. He felt a hand on his arm.

"You have to keep your cool," Troy warned him once again.

"I will. Let's go." Cole practically leaped out of the truck, and bounded up the stairs to the front door within seconds. He knocked on the door and waited. No one answered. Troy made a fist and pounded a few more times, much louder. Still, no one came to the door. Cole cupped his hands against the window next to the door and peeked inside.

"I don't think he's home," Cole said, as he looked around the yard.

"Let's check the barn out," he told Troy. They walked to the barn doors together. Troy pulled on the handle; it was locked.

"Troy, over here," Cole summoned him to come around to the side of the structure. Troy approached and asked, "What do you have?"

Cole pointed at the dirty window. "Is that the truck that was following us in Canada?" Cole asked.

Troy raised his hand and wiped the glass a little so he could see better. "It looks like it. I would be more positive if I could see the license plate," Troy answered. "Come on, let's get out of here. We don't have a search warrant. We'll come back later." Troy patted Cole on the back.

Cole bowed his head, closed his eyes and muttered, "I'll be back for you, you son of a bitch. I know it's you!" They drove away reluctantly.

Chapter 13

An hour later, Lucy felt a little more relaxed. She had taken a shower and put on sweats, then relaxed on her living room sofa, sipping a glass of white wine. She looked out the window at the driveway several times, waiting for Cole to arrive. She hoped he would come before darkness fell. She didn't like to be alone in the house at night, especially since she now knew someone was stalking her. Lucy stood and went to the back door. She looked down at the lock, just to make sure it was secured. She stared out at the water for a minute. *How beautiful the sunset is, with the orange and red colors,* she thought. She looked to her right toward the trees. A cold chill ran down her back and she rubbed her arms, trying to warm herself up.

She went back to the living room and sat down briefly. Lucy gulped the last of her wine, hoping it would calm her nerves. She walked to her kitchen counter and grabbed the bottle for a refill, almost dropping it when she saw a shadow out of the corner of her eye. Something or someone had passed by the living room window. She froze. Her heart jumped, feeling like it was in her throat. Her hands began to shake. She gently put the bottle down on the counter. *Did I just imagine that?* she thought. Lucy took a few steps back until her body hit the wall. Her eyes focused on the large window. *What weapons do I have? Was it Rodney? Think! He wouldn't harm me; I haven't done anything to give him cause.* She inhaled deeply then let it out. *This is crazy. I am not going to be a victim in my own home.*

Lucy timidly left her spot on the wall and slowly moved toward the door. She flicked on the outside porch light. She touched the door handle for a moment, then gripped it determinedly and unlocked it. She unhurriedly turned the knob, then closed her eyes for a second and bit her lower lip. *What are you going to do or say if he's there?* She opened the door and took a step outside. Her whole body was trembling with fear as she moved forward and stood on the porch. She looked to her right, then to her left. Nobody! She pulled her strength together and decided to ask, "Rodney, is that you? If it's you, please don't scare me. If you need something, tell me." She stood still, listening for anything, any movement. Nothing! Then she saw them. Wildflowers on the top step of her porch, tied with a yellow ribbon. She swallowed hard and picked up the flowers, keeping her eyes focused on the woods. She didn't see anyone.

"Thank you," she said a little louder, hoping that recognizing the flowers would make him happy. Lucy turned around and walked back inside. She locked the door immediately and walked to the kitchen, still frightened. She dropped the flowers on the table, disgusted, and stared at them trying to figure out what to do next. "Where are you, Cole? Please hurry!" she whispered.

***

Rodney made the decision to climb down from his hiding place. It had been almost an hour. He was heartbroken that Lucy hadn't collected the flowers. He had worked so hard to gather them for her. She had gone inside the house without even glancing at them. She was alone. *Maybe she didn't see them. I have to move them so she'll see them.* He strapped his bow around his body and crouched down near the bushes. *At least that fucking trooper isn't around,* he thought. Rodney surveyed the yard; no one was there. He stayed low and crossed the lawn. He stopped by the side of the house to catch his breath, then peeked down the porch. He could see his gift. Rodney ran up the stairs and went straight to the rocking chair. He ran past the bay window and down the porch stairs, pausing to put the flowers on the top step. He then hurried around the corner of the house. He stopped with his back against the building. Sweat dripped down his temples.

Rodney saw the porch light shine on the porch area and lawn. He waited, not moving a muscle, hoping she hadn't seen him. He sneaked a quick peek around the corner and saw that she was looking the opposite way, holding the flowers, the ends of the yellow ribbon around them dangling. He was surprised, and his heart swelled with joy. He held his breath in shock when he heard her mention his name. *She knows the flowers are from me!* His mouth opened; Rodney wanted to talk to her, but no words came out. He was too nervous, too scared of rejection. He wanted to tell her he would never intentionally scare her or harm her. He loved her; he would die for her. He heard her thank him for the wild blossoms. His heart bulged with pride. *She cares for me! She'll wear them in her hair tomorrow,* he thought.

Could she really love me as much as I love her? he thought. *Does she want to make love with me? What about the dog I injured? And the teddy bear? Oh, God! Am I in trouble? NO! I am not in trouble. That trooper doesn't have anything on me. I am innocent, and I am fine,* he thought. *It's the trooper's fault for Lucy not getting closer to me. She wants me. I won't be stopped! I will just have to get rid of that trooper!*

Rodney remained near Lucy's house for a few more minutes, but he was sure she was not coming back outside. He bent down low, ran, and returned to his hiding place up in the tree. He sat on the same branch that he had earlier, where he had a clear view of the cottage and the driveway. He would be patient. He was sure the trooper would appear sooner or later. Like a predator hunting another animal for food, Rodney watched for his prey. Quiet, resigned, and tireless in the hunt, Rodney would reap the rewards and get the prize.

Rodney zipped up his jacket all the way, chilled by a breeze from the north. He was still straddling the branch, where he could see any movement at the house. It was so quiet all you heard were the light sounds of the lake's waves, the hooting of an owl once in a while, and whispers of the leaves in the breeze.

Rodney's patience paid off. Suddenly he saw headlights coming up the driveway. He straightened his back against the trunk of the tree. He watched a truck park near the house, then saw Cole and another man get out of it. He reached into his case for an arrow, placed it carefully against the bowstring, and brought it to eye level. He pulled the arrow and the string back, holding them tightly. Rodney's aim toward his target was precise.

"I could kill both of you. You wouldn't have a chance. I could bring you down, right now," he snarled.

***

Lucy was still trembling when she heard the sound of Cole's truck. She marched to the window and pushed the curtain aside to make sure it was Cole. She felt a rush of relief. *Cole is here!* She dashed to the front door and unlocked it. She scurried outside on the porch, down the stairs, and into his arms. Lucy hugged Cole tightly.

"Hey! Are you okay?" Cole asked, with concern in his tone.

"He's here! He left me flowers again. I saw someone move on the porch," she replied in a shaky voice. He gently pushed her toward the house, wanting to keep holding her close. He nodded, then tilted his head toward the woods.

"Check it out," Cole told Troy. Troy walked toward the trees with his gun drawn in front of him.

Lucy stopped at the door to see what might happen, but Cole directed her inside. "Let's go inside, where it's safer. Troy will be right back. He's just going to check the surroundings," Cole said. They sat on the sofa and Cole took her hands in his. She could feel more tears stinging her eyes. She bowed her head just as one tear escaped and rolled down her cheek.

"Everything is fine. I'm here. Don't cry. He's not going to hurt you. Now, tell me what happened." Cole urged, wiping her tears away.

"I came home, took a shower, and had a glass of wine. I was in the kitchen when I saw someone go by on the porch, from the corner of my eye. So I went to see who it was, but there was no one there. I saw another bouquet of wild-flowers on the top step," she explained, and pointed toward the kitchen counter. Cole turned his head and looked at the bouquet, then nodded.

"It's okay. You are going to come stay with me until we apprehend him. Now, come on, up. Go pack a bag," he said. Cole stood up and led her to the bedroom.

***

Troy walked to the tree line with his gun aimed and ready. His eyes were darting from right to left for anything unusual, any sound or movement. He was careful with his footing as he moved slowly over the tall grass. Troy pushed through the bushes, then stopped with his back against a large oak tree. He scanned his surroundings and listened for any suspicious noises. His finger was on the trigger, ready to shoot. What he really wanted was arrest the bastard, throw him in jail, and let him rot for what he had done. He proceeded about ten feet to another oak tree. Troy didn't move for a minute; he closed his eyes momentarily, and held his breath as his adrenaline spiked. He could feel his heartbeat pounding against his chest. He sensed danger. Listened intently for any sound, he saw a couple leaves fall from above and hit the ground.

He looked up and saw a figure sitting on a branch overhead. Troy raised his firearm, but before he could shoot, he heard a swishing sound. Excruciating pain engulfed his chest, and he fell to the ground. As he fell, Troy pulled the trigger, firing two shots before he blacked out from the pain of his injuries.

***

Cole was sitting on Lucy's bed watching her pack a bag when he heard the gunshots. He sprang up, pulled his gun out of its holster, and ran toward the door.

"Call 911, and tell them to send backup. Stay inside and lock the door!" he shouted as he ran past Lucy. He cautiously moved in the direction of the shots.

"Troy! Are you all right?" he yelled and pushed the bushes aside with one hand. He crouched down to listen, and waited for his eyes to adapt to the darkness. *I need cover. Otherwise, I'm in big trouble,* he thought. There was a tree about twenty feet from him on his right. He rushed to it and squatted near the trunk. He surveyed the area, first looking to his right, then his left. Cole strained to hear any sounds, but there was dead silence. He moved onward to the next tree. He went down on one knee, his side against the trunk, taking a deep breath to calm himself. Cole peeked around the tree, scanning the area. His gun was held close to his chest, ready to fire. He whipped his head to the left when he thought he heard a muffled sound, but he didn't see anything.

He sprinted toward the sound, stopped, crouched low and concentrated on the noise. Time was passing, and he still didn't see Troy. Cole was worried about him—and also about Lucy being alone. Suddenly, he saw some movement about twenty yards away. *It's a man running away through the trees!*

"Freeze! Police! Stop right now! Rodney?!" he yelled. The man stopped, turned, then aimed and shot an arrow in a fraction of a second. It flew by Cole just as he ducked. He threw himself to the ground and rolled, ending in a crouch. He lifted the gun, zeroed in on the man, and pulled the trigger several times. He couldn't see him anymore, but got a glimpse of movement. "Troy?" he shouted, as he kept an eye out for the intruder. Cole crawled in the direction of the movement. Cole's eyes widened in fear for his friend when he saw him. Sitting back on his heels beside Troy, Cole placed his gun in his waistband. Troy was lying on his back, with an arrow sticking out of his chest. He was non-responsive and wasn't moving.

"Troy," Cole said sternly. Cole placed his fingers on the artery in Troy's neck. *Nothing! No pulse. Dear God! This cannot be happening.* Cole shook Troy firmly, holding him by the shoulders. His injured friend was totally limp, still not reacting—not even a twitch. Cole could hear sirens approaching.

"Troy, wake up, please," he pleaded. He then placed his hands together on Troy's chest and started CPR.

"Don't you die on me! Do you hear me?!" Cole yelled. Cole heard his name being shouted. He turned his head without stopping compressions on Troy's chest.

"Over here! I'm over here!" he screamed. Two officers came running through the trees.

"Get the EMTs here, fast! Hurry!" Cole screamed. He did not stop trying to revive Troy.

"Which way did he go?" another trooper asked. His face showed concern as he looked down at Troy.

"Straight ahead, about ten minutes ago," he motioned with his head in the direction for them to go.

"Catch that fucking bastard, and call for reinforcements," he said, his voice breaking. Tears clouded his vision. He was trying to bring Troy back to life. But he knew; Troy was gone.

***

Rodney didn't have a choice. He was not going to be caught. He watched the man with a gun walk into the tree line, in the vicinity of where Rodney sat in the tree. The man had a handgun, and Rodney was afraid for his life, He positioned his bow. *I don't know you, but you must be a friend of Cole. You must be looking for me.* Rodney tried not to move on the branch, not wanting to attract attention. The man was just below him. Rodney pulled the arrow back. He slowly took aim; when he moved, a couple of the branch's leaves dropped to the ground. Rodney didn't want to shoot the man with his arrow, and hoped he would just walk away. The man looked up and raised his firearm. *I've been found,* Rodney thought. Rodney let go of the arrow. It hit Troy directly in the chest. Troy pulled the trigger of his pistol; two bullets whizzed by Rodney. *I didn't have a choice,* Rodney thought. *I had to defend myself. I have done nothing wrong.*

Rodney climbed down the tree quickly and stood by the man's side. He probably couldn't have asked for a better target. Rodney figured he'd hit him through the heart, or very close to it. He wasn't moving. Rodney bent down and picked up the man's gun, then placed it carefully inside his coat pocket. He heard branches being crushed from not too far away. Rodney sprinted in the opposite direction of the man he'd noticed coming his way; it was that trooper named Cole. Cole ran in Rodney's direction. Rodney could see Cole getting closer. *I might get my chance to get rid of him after all,* he thought. He heard Cole yelling at him. *How did he know my name?* Cole screamed at him to stop, but he wasn't afraid. Rodney reached into his case and took out another arrow. He turned halfway, and let it rip through the air toward his pursuer. He started to run away from Cole without looking back. *Run! Run faster,* he thought. Rodney turned his head to take a peek. Cole had stopped pursuing him. He tried to decide where to hide to get away. He knew these woods like the back of his hand, had been brought up on these trails. Rodney knew every hiding place and every tree position. He also knew the cavalry was probably on their way to try and capture him, now that he had killed a man. Rodney was breathing hard. He stopped and glanced back while trying to catch his breath. He bent at the waist, putting his hands on his knees. His eyes swept the area. *They all think I'm going to flee to this forest and hide. They'll have hundreds of cops roaming the region. What am I going to do? Well, they're all wrong! All I have to do is lose my trail.*

Rodney turned his head and grinned smugly. He backtracked his steps to head for the water. He had hurried enough to reach it before everyone arrived on his heels. He followed the edge of the waves of the lake until he could see Lucy's cottage. He hid in the bushes again and watched her place. She wasn't anywhere in sight. Since the darkness would conceal him, he decided to move close to the house. Rodney sprinted toward the bungalow and stopped at the far wall. Sweat was dripping down his brow. His radar was on high alert. There was no noise, and Cole was nowhere to be seen. There was only one police car parked in front, but no troopers were visible.

Rodney knew the house pretty well; the front porch had a wood skirting all the way around the perimeter of the structure. The house was held up by cement blocks, so this was the ideal place. *Genius!* He grinned. He crouched down near the back of the house and pulled a wood panel from an opening of the foundation. He crawled under the cottage. It was cramped, only about three feet high, but it was the ideal hiding place for now. *I can be right here under their noses, and they won't know it. I can hear the details of their search*, he thought. He chuckled quietly. Rodney replaced the boards exactly as they were before so they wouldn't detect anything out of the ordinary. *I might as well make myself comfortable, since I might be here a while*, he thought. He crept on hands and knees toward the front of the house. Rodney could hear Lucy's voice and footsteps up above. Sirens were blaring closer and closer to his position.

Chapter 14

Lucy stood on the front porch with a shawl wrapped around her shoulders, trying to calm herself and take the chill away. She felt helpless as she watched Cole run out the door with his gun dawn. She called for backup immediately, just as he had told her to do, but that seemed such a long time ago—even though it had only been ten minutes. She couldn't stay inside like he had told her to do; she needed to know what was going on. Lucy pulled her wrap tighter around her body, unable to get the coldness away from her body. *Maybe I should go see what is going on.* She stared at the woods, waiting. She paced back and forth from one end of the veranda to the other. Lucy stopped when she heard the sirens coming her way.

Three Maine State Police cars stopped in haste. Several men in uniforms jumped out, armed and ready for anything.

"They went that way; hurry, Cole and I heard gunshots," she screamed at them, pointing toward the trees. Two of them disappeared behind the trees.

"Hi, my name is Captain Richard Collins," one man said, shaking her hand. "Let's go inside until we know more. It's not safe to stay out here," he said and guided her back inside. She walked to a chair in the living room and sat down without a word.

"Okay. Now, what's the situation?" he asked. "Tell me what's going on," he instructed. He eyed the outside through the living room window.

"Troy went into the woods looking for a man named Rodney, who has been stalking me for weeks. Then Cole heard gunshots, and he ran out to help. That's all I know so far," she explained. Lucy could barely speak. Her voice was shaky, and her eyes were filled with tears.

"Stay right here; don't move," he ordered. She watched him walk outside. She could hear him talking on his radio to the other troopers. Lucy tried to understand what was going on. He went to his patrol car and pulled out his shotgun. Her mind went crazy thinking about what might be happening. Was Cole okay? Was he hurt? She could hear the noise of more sirens coming toward the house. She watched from the front window. More officers and an ambulance had arrived. She observed as the EMT took out an emergency bodyboard and medical bags. They swung them over their shoulders and ran in the direction where she thought Troy and Cole were. Someone was hurt.

"Oh, God! Please don't let it be Cole," she prayed out loud. Her whole body was shaking from fright. Lucy watched as officers swarmed the perimeter of the woods, one after another. She noticed the captain radioing orders and directing his people in searching different sections. She needed to find out what was going on. Lucy walked out to the porch door when one of the officers said, "Please stay inside, it's not safe out here." He put his hand up to stop her from going any further.

"Please, I just want to know what's going on. Cole Baker is my boyfriend. Could you locate him, find out if he's injured? Please, help me," she pleaded with him.

He looked at her with sympathetic eyes and said, "I think he's fine. I'll get the captain. He might be able to tell you more." He had just walked down the stairs when she saw a figure come out of the bushes.

"Cole!" she screamed. Lucy raced toward him, bypassing the troopers. She heard someone shout, "Miss, come back here!" The trooper tried to grab her arm and missed. She kept running toward her love, Cole.

"It's okay," she heard someone yell back. Wild horses couldn't keep her away. With her arms opened wide, she jumped into Cole's arms and hugged him tightly.

"Thank God! Are you okay? I was so scared," she said and looked at him.

"I'm all right," he answered in a low voice. She saw the blood on his shirt and her mouth opened in surprise.

Cole took her hand in his when he saw her reaction to the blood. He said, "It's not my blood. It's Troy's," She stared into his eyes. She knew—Troy was the one who was hurt, otherwise he would be by Cole's side—he was dead. She could see it in Cole's face. He shook his head sadly, confirming it.

"Oh, no! No, it isn't true," she cried out. Lucy sobbed. Cole just shook his head.

"I couldn't save him," he said in a hollow tone. Lucy's heart broke to pieces at the thought of him losing his best friend. Cole wiped his tears away.

"I swear, Lucy, if I catch the son of a bitch, I'll kill him with my bare hands," he told her with his teeth clenched. She wrapped her arms around his waist and pulled him toward the cottage. Cole trudged back inside the house, his head held low. He went straight to the bedroom and slammed the door hard. Lucy didn't speak, she just sat beside him on the bed. He put his hands over his face and cried like a baby. Loud sobs echoed in the room. She didn't say a word, she just rubbed his back gently. Lucy was trying to be strong for him, but it was futile. Tears streamed down her cheeks like a waterfall, too. Cole eventually explained what had happened to Troy, and how he couldn't do anything to help him.

About half an hour later, Cole got control of his emotions. His eyes and nose were red, and his face wet with many tears. He stood and walked to the window. Raindrops began to fall against the window pane. Cole stared straight ahead, not moving a muscle. His head was bowed, his arms hanging limply beside him. Lucy walked over to him and wrapped her arms around his waist, then laid her head against his back. She felt him tense up.

"I'm so sorry, Cole. What can I do to help?" she asked, trying to ease his feeling of distress.

"There nothing you can do," he answered sadly.

They didn't move from their spot for a minute, Then she let go of him and said, "Come on, take off that shirt and wash off. I'll get you a clean shirt. Come on," she cajoled very softly. Lucy escorted him to the bathroom, and he did as she asked without a single word. He washed Troy's blood off his hands and body.

"Here, take this," she told him, after he had changed into one of his T-shirts previously left behind at her house. She had found two Tylenol in the medicine cabinet, and offered them to him with a glass of water. He took them from her and swallowed them without protest. She could hear the rain battering against the roof, and sounds of thunder from afar.

"Thank you. I'm going to have one of the officers take you to my house. You'll be safe there until we find the son of a bitch," Cole said. He gently took Lucy in his arms and kissed her forehead.

"Cole, I'm not going anywhere. I'm not going to flee my home because of him. Plus, I feel safe here, with all the police personnel around. I'll be fine, and I'm not leaving you alone," she told him sternly. She looked up at him, and he nodded.

"All right. I have a few calls to make, and then I need to see where the search is going. I need to talk to the guys," he said. Cole glanced toward the window, where he could see the assembly of the police force being put together to search for the fugitive.

"This rain is not helping at all. It's probably going to erase any evidence of footprints, and the dogs won't be able to retrieve his scent. *Damn!*" he said harshly.

"Don't worry, they'll catch him. If not tonight, tomorrow. What are you going to do?" Lucy asked. She was worried about Cole.

"First I'm going to talk to Captain Collins, and see what they found so far. Then we'll see," he told her. "Please promise me you'll stay inside, I don't want you outside. I don't know where he went, or what he would do now if he's cornered and armed. He stole Troy's gun," he said. Cole pulled her into his arms and kissed her on the lips. She held on to him for a few extra seconds, and then watched him stride out the front door.

***

Cole was determined to find the bastard, if it was the last thing he ever did. He had such mixed emotions. He was filled with sorrow for his friend and hatred for Rodney, who killed him. He went to the truck to gathered his rain gear and a backpack that he kept for emergencies. It contained food, water, his bulletproof vest, a compass, and a first aid kit, among other things. Cole rushed under a tent that the emergency personnel had erected for shelter. The whole driveway was swarming with policemen, the SWAT team, and EMTs. More police personnel were already hunting for Rodney in the woods.

"Captain, what can I do?" Cole asked, walking toward him. Collins glanced away from the map he was studying and placed it down on the table. He walked to meet Cole and pulled him to the side, away from the others.

"Cole, the best thing for you to do right now is nothing. Internal affairs will be coming by for your statement, and I need you here. Why don't you keep your girlfriend company?" he suggested. He folded his arms across his chest.

"Come on, Captain. You know Troy was my best friend. You have to let me search for this bastard," Cole protested, putting on his rain jacket.

"That is precisely why I can't allow you out there. You can stay here and monitor the hunt, but that's all—at least until we know more about what's happening. That's final," he sternly told Cole, and strolled back to the table.

Cole stood immobile, stunned that he couldn't participate in the son of a bitch's apprehension. He sighed heavily, unhappy that he had been put on the sidelines. He knew his captain would not change his mind; it was policy, after all. He walked back to the house and went inside.

Lucy was making coffee in the kitchen. When Cole came in, she asked, "So, what's going on?" Lucy poured a cup of coffee and handed it to Cole, then sat down on the stool next to him.

"The captain won't let me go out to search for the bastard, so I'm stuck here," he told her then took a sip of his coffee

"I'm really sorry about Troy. I feel partly responsible, because if it weren't for me, he would still be alive." Lucy's voice trembled and her eyes filled with tears again, so she looked away.

"Lucy, look at me," Cole said. He raised his hand and gently turned her head to face him. She lowered her eyes and stared at the floor.

"It's not your fault. You are not responsible for *any* of it. Do you hear me? Rodney is the one stalking you, and he murdered Troy. Now come here, and give me a hug," he said. She stood up and let Cole's arms encircle her, standing between his legs.

"Hmm!" he said and kissed the top of her head. He could feel her body heat; it warmed the chill he felt deep inside.

"I love you, and he will not hurt you while I'm here," he reassured her, holding her against his chest.

"I love you, too," she answered, and kissed him on the lips.

"I'm glad you're here; now I feel much safer. Let me make you something to eat. It's going to be a long night," Lucy said and pulled away from his embrace. She walked around the counter, opened the refrigerator, and took out cold cuts and bread to make him a sandwich.

***

Rodney lay on his back near the middle cement blocks of the home's foundation, which ran near the front porch. He tried to catch his breath and calm his nerves. It was raining, and the water kept dripping down from the cracks in between the wood panels of the porch. The water turned the dirt underneath him into mud, so he turned over on his belly and pulled up the hood of his jacket. Through the gaps in the wood skirts, he could see the officers moving around. He also heard the policemen talking about him, and their plans to apprehend him. Rodney chuckled quietly every time he heard his name mentioned; that he was right under their noses gave him a thrill. His bow was next to him. *I am so clever, to think of this hideout,* he thought. *They will never suspect I'm here.*

Rodney heard Lucy's voice through the floorboards. It was masked by all the noise outside, but he knew it was her. He could hear light footsteps above him, and longed to go hold her. No woman had ever been so nice to him, and he wanted her. *She belongs to me. She's mine. I want to spend the rest of my life with her. I love her,* he thought. He wondered how it would feel to embrace her in his arms, to touch her skin softly or kiss her. A surge of jealousy invaded his body when he heard Cole walking around, talking to his Lucy Rodney dug his fingers into the dirt, trying not to think of the other man being near her.

Two hours had passed by when his attention was distracted by barking dogs. He heard someone yell, "Bring the dogs! Maybe we'll get lucky, and they can pick up the scent before the rain washes it all away." Rodney crawled forward and pulled himself closer to the wood skirt to look through the crack. He spied two officers with K9 dogs disembarking from an SUV. The dogs were sniffing around on the ground, pulling their masters in different directions. He watched one officer put what looked like one of his garments from work to the animal's nose. *Yes, that's my uniform,* he thought. The dogs inhaled his smell, and headed toward the tree line. Rodney grinned at how idiotic they were. "I'm not in the woods. I'm right here," he said in a low voice.

When nightfall came, Rodney was soaked and cold, but the rain had finally stopped. He noticed several vehicles had left the area, and others arrived. Two police officers walked toward him. They stood no more than ten feet from the porch skirt, talking to each other. Rodney grasped his gun tightly in his right hand and pointed it at the state troopers, ready to shoot them if they discovered him. The man in charge was talking to the other one.

"There's not much more we can do tonight. We might as well send most of them home, and start fresh at dawn. It's too dangerous for them in the woods at night. They don't know the area that well, and they have no cover if they're attacked. We can leave a handful of officers here overnight in case he comes back, but I doubt that he will tonight," Rodney heard the captain say.

"You're probably right. We'll have more manpower coming from the state tomorrow. We have roadblocks at all major roadways, and surveillance on the farmhouse. They can patrol the streets tonight; maybe he'll do something stupid and we'll get him then," the other answered.

"Yeah, but I was told the bastard knows these woods like the back of his hand. He's not that bright, though. He'll eventually screw up, and we'll apprehend him. All right, I'll see you in the morning," the captain said, and walked away. Rodney watched them leave, relieved they hadn't seen him. He put his gun in his back pocket and wormed his way back to his original spot near the back of the porch, where it was darker. His stomach growled, so he dug into his bag for one of his power bars and a bottle of water. Rodney ate while he watched most of the policemen depart. He needed to get some shut-eye; otherwise, he wouldn't be able to think straight tomorrow. He pulled his bag close and placed it under his head as a pillow. He took the gun from his back pocket and held it on his chest in both hands, then closed his eyes and fell into a light sleep.

Chapter 15

Lucy and Cole lay on the bed in each other's arms trying to get some sleep, but it was impossible. Lucy glanced over to the night table, where Cole's gun was resting. It was not far from his hand, ready to bring Rodney down. The captain had come to the bungalow to inform them the search for Rodney was suspended for the night, and that they would resume the manhunt in the early hours of the morning. Several men were posted around the perimeter of the grounds and near the house for their protection, but Lucy was still shaken by the events of the day.

"Why don't you close your eyes? I'm right here, and I have your back. He won't dare come near this house tonight—and if he does, we'll take care of him," Cole told Lucy. He pulled the blanket upwards to cover her shoulder and squeezed her nearer to his body.

"I know. I'm so grateful to have you here. I just... I can't believe this is happening because of me," Lucy answered softly. She nuzzled her face into his shoulder.

"He dug his own grave. He's probably far away by now, lost somewhere in the woods. They'll catch him," Cole said confidently.

"You're the one who needs to fall asleep, not me, I can nap during the day tomorrow," Lucy said. She placed her hand under his T-shirt and rubbed his hard abs.

"I'm not tired—and if you keep massaging my belly, there's no way I'm going to sleep," Cole answered, so she kept her hand still.

"I'm sorry. I just thought it would relax you," Lucy said, and started to pull away. Cole kept his arm secured around her waist, not letting her move. He grabbed her with both hands and pulled her on top of him. She was inches from his face; she smiled at him wickedly, then brushed her lips on his mouth, barely touching it. She licked his upper lip with her tongue, then pulled away.

"I definitely don't want to sleep now," Cole whispered. He grabbed the bottom edges of her blouse and lifted it up. She could feel his hands roaming up and down her back, then unfastening her bra. He threw it on the floor. He looked up at her bare breasts and moaned. She laid her erect nipples against his chest, her core demanding more from him.

"I'll get you to sleep one way or another," Lucy murmured in his ear. He growled at her as she lifted his shirt over his head. She moved her breasts downward against his bare skin, her whole body coming alive as she felt him grow underneath her. She leaned down and kissed him as if it might be their last night together. A wave of ecstasy was mounting as her hands began to unbuckle his jeans.

***

Cole woke up to the sound of car doors slamming near the house. He turned his head toward the window and squinted at the morning light shining through. Lucy's head was resting on his naked chest, her arm draped across his belly. He eased himself out of bed without waking her. He found his jeans at the foot of the bed and slipped them on, then his T-shirt. He grabbed his gun and placed it in his waistband. Cole took one last glimpse at Lucy lying in the bed, sleeping so peacefully without a worry. She was so beautiful with her tousled hair half over her face. His heart warmed up at the sight of her. He would protect her from that bastard, even if he lost his own life doing it. He loved her to death, and as soon as this ordeal was over, he was going to ask her to marry him. Cole realized that even though he had only known her for a short time, he cherished her and didn't want to leave her side. She brought more joy to his life than he'd ever thought possible.

He tiptoed out of the room and closed the door behind him. He strolled through the house and stepped outside on the veranda, then walked over to the crowd of police officers gathered near the command unit. Cole approached one of the commanders of the Maine State Troopers, who was pouring a cup of coffee.

"Sir, my name is Cole Baker. I was the one who found Trooper Levy. I was wondering what the latest news was about the manhunt," he asked. A wave of sorrow passed through him at the mention of his friend's name. He clenched his jaw to prevent his tears from falling.

"Nice to meet you. It's not looking good. The dogs weren't able to track his scent yesterday because of the rain. We didn't get any hits from the roadblocks. The SWAT team has been going house to house. We're following all possible leads we receive. We will probably be moving our command center closer to town, and widening the search if we don't catch him in the next day or so. I know it's hard, but we'll get him," he answered. He nodded at Cole, and extended his hand to shake. Cole's hand.

"Thank you, sir, I'll let you go back to work, I appreciate your time," Cole told him. He raked his hand through his hair and looked around the area at all his fellow officers, who were trying desperately to capture this son of a bitch. He talked to a few colleagues briefly, and walked back inside the cottage to go check on Lucy.

***

Rodney smiled from ear to ear while he listened to the commander explain to Cole his plans to arrest him. He giggled silently to himself as he took it all in. He would be able to move out of this hole if they moved out closer to town. He turned over on his back with his eyes closed, thinking about what his next move should be. *How do I regain Lucy's trust and love?* he thought. When Rodney opened his eyes, he saw a small framed door on the ceiling between the beams. It was probably about two feet by two and a half feet. He had not seen it before because of the darkness of the night.

Perfect! I can slide through that opening to escape if they find my hideout. He wondered if he'd be able to open it. He reached up and touched the trap door lightly with his fingertips. *What room of the house is this?* This could be his way out without being seen by the cops. He counted the joists from the end of the house to the back. He tried to center himself and compare the small door to the floor plan in his head, figuring out what room he had seen Lucy in through the windows, and how that related to where he was at the moment. He determined that the door was probably in the kitchen; whoever needed access to the crawlspace for repairs would find this the easiest way underneath. Rodney bit his dirty fingernails as he examined the door.

He knew Lucy was still in the house, but he hadn't seen or heard her outside this morning. He needed to find a way to open this door and peek inside without being detected. Rodney decided he would have to wait until both Lucy and that cop were out of the house before he made his move. He heard his stomach growl from hunger. He placed his hand on his stomach and rubbed it. Rodney had no food left; he had eaten all his provisions, and he was thirsty, too. Maybe he could sneak into the house tonight and grab a few supplies so he'd be able to hole up for the next few days. He had to make a plan.

***

Lucy spent most of the day making coffee and sandwiches for the troopers who guarded her home. It was late afternoon when she opened her refrigerator door and realized there wasn't much food left to cook for supper. She needed to go to town to get groceries. She had been cooped up for the last two days, anyway. A ride away from this house would do her good. She went outside to find Cole.

"Cole? Cole!" she yelled. He was standing on the front steps. She raised her hand and waved at him to come to her. She watched him excuse himself from the group of his colleagues, and he came running to her. He gently kissed her lips and stood beside her.

"What does my love need, that she is screaming at me across the way?" he teased. He put his hands on her hips and pulled her close.

Lucy put her hands flat on his chest and giggled. "I wanted to know if you would take me down to Houlton. I really have to get a few things from the grocery store." Cole frowned. She could tell he didn't want to leave.

"Come on, you and I need a break from this," and she pointed at the surrounding throng of people, "anyway—and we wouldn't be gone long," she wheedled. Cole didn't move; he just stared at her, then looked at the crowd around them.

"Please? Otherwise, we'll be eating canned ravioli," she joked. He laughed out loud at her response and nodded.

"Okay, you're right. Go get your purse. I'll get the truck. I really don't want to eat canned ravioli for supper," he said, laughing. He slapped her butt as she walked away. Within minutes, they were sitting in his truck on their way to the supermarket in Houlton.

***

Rodney was watching everything that was going on in front of him through the cracks when he heard a familiar voice. It was hers! It was like a bird singing in his ears. He looked up at the ceiling when he heard other footsteps on the steps. His jaw tightened, and his hands dug into the dirt when he listened to them talking so sweetly to each other. Jealousy invaded his body. He heard her go into the house, then come back out and lock the door. He watched her get in the truck with Cole, and watched them leave.

Now was his chance to get into the house. He wiggled his way in the dirt to the trap door about ten feet away. Rodney lay there for a moment, listening for any noises inside. He didn't hear a sound. *Good, the coast is clear*, he thought. He reached up and pushed hard on the panel. The door swung upward quietly. There was no lock. He smiled, opening it wide enough that he could kneel with his head above the floor and check out the surroundings. His eyes darted back and forth. He was in the kitchen. He lifted the door a little more. He popped his head up a little more and looked around again. He was underneath the kitchen table. Rodney finally shoved the door all the way open and climbed out from underneath the house. He pulled the trooper's gun from his waistband and held it tight in his right hand, ready for anything that might arise. He made his way to the fridge. He was starving. Rodney hadn't eaten anything in the last twenty-four hours except a granola bar. He grabbed the handle and swung it open while keeping an eye on the front door. *Not much left in this fridge; no wonder she went to grocery store*, he thought. He did notice an apple, which he reached over and snatched it off the shelf, taking a big bite of it immediately. He grabbed a half-eaten sandwich and a bottle of water from the middle shelf. He stuffed them into his pockets while still chewing on his apple.

Rodney walked around the house cautiously, making sure to avoid the windows so no one would see him. He ran to the far wall and poked his head into one of the rooms to see what was in it; it was her bedroom. The bed was covered with a blue comforter, and matching curtains were hung on the windows, which were closed. He took a step inside and inhaled her fragrance, lingering in the air. He took a step to his right, and he was standing in front of a tall bureau. He gently touched the bottles of perfume sitting on top of it.

He picked up one bottle, a perfume called Angel, brought it to his nose and inhaled. "Mmm!" he said out loud. He loved the scent. He placed the core of his eaten apple on the top of the bureau. He then opened the first drawer of the bureau. Rodney's eyebrows lifted, and he licked his lips. He picked up a pair of red lace panties, then smirked as he folded them and put them in his jacket pocket. He pushed the drawer closed and proceeded to look around the bedroom. He noticed a framed picture of Lucy near a model boat on one of the shelves on the wall. *Nice picture! I'll take it with me, so I can look at her later.* He shoved that into his pocket, too. Rodney searched one room after another quickly. He didn't want to stay too long, so ten minutes later, he walked back to the kitchen.

He bent down and jumped back into the opening under the table, but not before he saw a blackboard on the wall with a grocery list written on it. He moved toward it and picked up the chalk, then wrote a note in the corner for Lucy. Rodney put the chalk back where he had found it, then turned and went back to the opening. He crawled down to his hiding place under the house, carefully closing the trap door behind him. He got on all fours and found his place in the darkest area, toward the back of the house, so he wouldn't be detected. Rodney took her underwear from his pocket and rubbed it against his cheek. An hour went by. He ate some of the leftover sandwich and closed his eyes, trying to take a nap while thinking of his love.

It was late afternoon when he was startled awake by the sound of a car door being shut near him. He listened as his eyes strained to see through the cracks of the foundation paneling. It was Lucy! She was giggling loudly. He heard footsteps above him, then he heard it: a barking dog. He saw the shadow of the animal near the front porch sniffing around on the ground. Shit! They had picked up the animal he thought was dead. He slowly removed his gun from his waistband and held it pointed toward the front of the house. He aimed the firearm in the direction of the dog. *This time, I'll make sure you're dead. I won't let you bite me again.*

"Come on, King. Come inside," Lucy's yelled from the porch steps. He watched as the dog left his spot by the skirt. Rodney heard the dog run up the stairs and the door close. He was gone; Rodney lowered his handgun and felt a sense of relief pass over him. *I'm still safe, but I'll have to keep an eye out for that fucking dog.* He didn't put the weapon away. He just placed it on the ground next to him, so he had access to it if he needed it in a hurry.

Chapter 16

The veterinarian had called Cole when he and Lucy were in town. He told Cole that King was ready to go home and was to be discharged, so he could pick him up anytime. It brought a smile on Cole's face thinking about having King home. They went to the hospital before going home. When they arrived at Lucy's place, she opened the back door of his truck to let King out. She grabbed the two small bags and carried them inside, while Cole went to the command post to see about any progress. She walked into the house and dropped her bags on the kitchen table. She decided to change into sweats before starting supper. She walked to her bedroom and opened the top drawer of her bureau. She tilted her head and grinned at the apple core on top of her dresser. "My dearest Cole, you need to learn to pick up after yourself," she said aloud and shook her head as she put sweatpants and a T-shirt on. She picked up the leftover apple core and dropped it in the wastebasket next to her, then returned to the kitchen.

Lucy reached up and opened the cupboard, then took out two bowls. She placed them on the counter and filled them up, one with water and the other with some dog food she had bought at the market after the vet called. She bent down and placed the bowls on the floor near the wall. She pulled the contents of her bags out and put them away in the cupboard or refrigerator. She placed a dozen eggs on one of the shelves in the fridge while she scanned the others.

"Gee! I thought I had a leftover sandwich, but I must be wrong. Cole probably ate it," Lucy said out loud and smiled.

She glanced down for a moment and watched King eat his meal. *Thank God he feels better.* She decided to prepare a hearty dinner, since they really hadn't been able to have a meal together the last few days. It would be nice to have some time together. She unwrapped two steaks and placed them on a plate. She added several different spices to a bowl and mixed it together, then rubbed it on the steaks to let them absorb the flavors. Lucy peeled potatoes next, and wrapped them in foil so she could put them on the barbecue. She heard the front door open and smiled as she watched Cole walk inside.

"Hey, Sweetheart. I decided to make steaks for supper. Is that okay?" Lucy asked as he approached her. He gave her a kiss on the back of the neck, and wrapped his arms around her waist. He turned her to face him.

"Why don't we skip dinner, and I'll have you instead," he whispered in her ear as he nibbled on her earlobe. She moaned quietly.

"Yes, but—" She didn't get to finish her sentence; Cole kissed her passionately, all the while pressing his body against hers. She heard King growl then bark twice. He sat next to their legs. Lucy and Cole looked down at him.

"You jealous, boy? What's the matter? Be quiet, and go lay down," Cole said playfully, and pointed to the carpet by the front door. King turned around and obeyed his master, but not without barking once again. They both laughed.

"Now, where were we?" Cole asked.

She picked up the potatoes from the counter and placed them in his hands, then told him, "You were just going to put these on the barbecue outside, while I make a salad."

He stuck out his lower lip at her and frowned. He marched toward the door and said, "Come on King, she doesn't want us in the kitchen," he said, and both disappeared behind the door.

Lucy watched the policemen outside from her kitchen window as she chopped lettuce and tomatoes. There weren't too many left in the area. Most of them had gone home, to resume the search in the morning, or had been reassigned farther down the road. She was happy to not be alone until this guy was caught. The only good thing that had come out of this was she had a chance to get closer to Cole. Her eyes welled with tears as she thought of the burial services tomorrow. It was going to be a very stressful and sad day for everyone who knew Troy. King's barking brought her back to her senses. Lucy shook her head, trying not to think about tomorrow's horrible event, and focused on cutting her vegetables for supper.

***

Cole lit the barbecue and placed the potatoes on the grill. He closed the cover and turned to look at King; the dog was fidgeting like a toddler, was running up and down the veranda. He growled, but didn't leave the porch area.

"King, stop it. Be quiet; sit," Cole ordered. He went to stroke King's head.

"Stay; I'll be right back," Cole told King as he re-entered the house. He went to the fridge, swung open the door and picked up a Corona. He took a big gulp.

"Do you want a beer, Sweetie?" Cole asked. He leaned against the doorframe and watched her finish cutting up the salad. He admired her every move. She was so pretty with her auburn hair tied up in a bun.

"In a moment. I'm almost done here. Why don't you go sit outside? I'll be along in a minute," she answered as she chopped the tomatoes. She continued chopping, so he decided to wait on the porch.

"Okay, I'll be outside if you need me," he said and went back out to sit on one of the rocking chairs. He rocked idly, his beer in his hand. His thoughts wandered. He didn't like being alone anymore, especially since Troy had died. It had taken a piece of his heart when he realized Troy was gone. And now he was afraid he might lose Lucy to this maniac. Cole's eyes teared up, and a tear fell from the corner of his eye. He raised his hand and wiped it away. He lifted his beer up to the sky and said, "To you, my dear friend; friends for life." He turned his head once again to look at King, sitting by his chair. His ears were perked up, and his eyes were darting around the property.

"I know you remember what happened over there in the woods, boy. Don't worry; we'll get the son of a bitch for you," he told King as he stroked his back. The dog stood up and barked a few times.

"Ready for the steak?" Lucy asked. He turned to look as she was pushing the screen door with one shoulder. She came out on the porch holding a plate with the two steaks in one hand and a pair of prongs in the other. Cole stood up from his chair to help her. He grabbed the plate and utensil from her.

"I'll cook them," he announced to her. He put the plate next to the barbe-cue and opened the lid with the other hand.

"Great! Then I'll go set the table, and we'll be all set. When the steaks are done, bring them in, okay?" she told him as Lucy turned around and headed back inside, smiling.

"No problem, anything else you need?" he asked, taking the steaks off the plate and dropping them on the grill.

"No, that's it, Sweetie," she answered, and disappeared inside. Cole's stom-ach growled as he flipped the steaks. The steaks sizzled, and the aroma made him hungry. Finally, they were cooked, and he took them off the grill. He took a few steps toward the door, but noticed King was pacing the porch and sniffing the deck again.

"Come on boy, let's go in! I'll give you the bone," he told the dog, holding the door open with his left hand. The dog looked up and barked.

"Come on!" Cole told him once again. This time, the dog came forward and entered the house.

***

Rodney held his breath as he listened to them talk. He didn't move a mus-cle, and his ears strained to catch every word. He heard the dog bark several times. He tightened his grip on his gun, hoping he wouldn't be discovered. Rodney exhaled deeply after he heard footsteps leaving the veranda area and go-ing inside. He was especially relieved when Cole told his mutt to come inside. He shoved his hand into his pocket to grab the remaining piece of the stale sandwich he had picked up from the refrigerator. The aroma of those steaks made him hungry. He bit into it with ferocity and chewed. He was still safe! His sight was riveted on the last few troopers who were still hanging around in the yard. Hopefully they would leave soon, so he could get the hell out of this filthy place that had become his hideaway for the last few days.

He had to be vigilant; if that mutt smelled his scent, he would be in big trouble. Rodney rammed the last bite in his mouth, chewed and swallowed. Even now his stomach was tender from hunger, but there was nothing he could do. He crawled to the back of the house near the opening to see if he could hear the conversations and maybe get some kind of information on the troopers' search. He raised himself up on one knee and placed his right ear close to the opening. He could hear Lucy and Cole talking, walking around the floor up above. He heard what sounded like they were dragging chairs. They were sitting down at the dinner table. They were right above him, just inches away! He could hear them talking about their meal. He simpered, pleased with himself that he had the advantage of hearing all their secrets.

Suddenly he overheard Cole mention that the commander of the SWAT team and other agencies would be leaving the area the next day, to relocate and extend their search elsewhere. He bit his fingernails and a self-congratulatory, smug little smile appeared on his face. He had beaten them all, and he would have his beloved one after all. He listened as the talked about the procession being organized for Troy's funeral the following day.

He listened for about an hour, racking up information as the time passed by. Finally, a sense of disgust invaded him. Rodney realized Lucy and Cole were no longer talking. He could hear movement and moaning coming from above. *Was he holding her, kissing her? How dare he touch her!* Rodney squeezed his hands tightly into fists and hit the dirt several times to vent his anger. He moved away from the sounds, crawling toward the other end of the foundation. He put his arms around his knees, curling into a fetal position, and didn't budge.

Rodney closed his eyes firmly and clenched his teeth. He was trying to muffle the sounds he heard by gritting his teeth. He should burst through that trap door and surprise them. He could shoot *him* dead, and afterward Lucy would be his. *She belongs to me!* He kept repeating in his mind. Rodney shook his head from side to side furiously. *I will find you when you're alone, then I'll talk to you, make you understand how much I love you—but not now. There are too many people around; I have to be patient. My time will come, and I will be happy.*

He had to find a way to get rid of Cole. Rodney shoved his hand into his pocket and retrieved Lucy's underwear. He held it in his hand looking at the delicate lace. He imagined her wearing it. He raised the panties to his nose and inhaled deeply. He could smell the floral scent of her perfume. He brought his hand down and held the underwear near his heart. Rodney lay in the dirt on his side, still gripping his lacy souvenir with one hand and the gun with the other. He closed his eyes and waited for sleep to come. Rodney hoped the nightmare he'd been through the last few days would turn into a sweet dream of Lucy.

***

Lucy woke up in the middle of the night, darkness all around her. She glanced at the only light in the room, which was her alarm clock. It was four thirty in the morning. She didn't want to disturb Cole, sleeping soundly next to her. She pulled the covers up to her neck to try to warm her chilled body. Her whole body was shivering from being cold. A wave of nausea passed through her. Her stomach felt as if it was ready to explode. She didn't move. She just held on to the covers and shut her eyes tightly, praying the queasiness would pass. *What the hell did I eat? Am I getting the flu?* she thought. A half hour later, she had to get up because she was afraid she might vomit in bed. She flung off the covers and ran for the bathroom. She bent at the waist, lifted the toilet seat, braced one hand on the side and started to gag. Her free hand grabbed her hair to pull it back just in time, an instant before she vomited into the bowl.

She sat down on the floor, her hands hugging the toilet. Nausea invaded her body. She sat there in silence. Minutes passed, and she still didn't dare move when she felt a hand stroke her shoulder. A soft voice said, "Babe, what the matter? Are you okay? Let me help you."

His strong arms slipped under her armpits and lifted her up. She stood up just as her whole body rejected the idea, a wave of queasiness overcoming her. She quickly turned toward the toilet bowl once again. Everything left hurled itself out of her stomach. Tears stung her eyes. *What the hell is the matter with me? Why am I so sick? What made me so sick?*

"Oh, dear. Babe, let me help you," Cole said. She noticed he had grabbed the towel off the counter and held it under the cold water faucet. He wrung the excess water out and came toward her. He gently washed Lucy's face and smiled at her.

"Feeling better?" he asked. She saw concern in his eyes as he frowned in worry. She just nodded at him.

"Let's go back to bed. I'll get you a bowl in case you get sick again," he told

132

her and helped her up once again. This time, she was feeling much better. He placed his arm around her waist and held her close to him as she took shaky steps out of the bathroom. He guided her to the bed, pulled the covers back, and she lay down. He pulled the covers way up to her neck, tucked her in, and leaned forward to kiss her forehead. Lucy closed her eyes, hoping she wouldn't be sick again; she just wanted to fall asleep.

"Babe, I got you a bowl, and a little ginger ale if you get thirsty. Why don't you try to sleep? If you need me, I'm right here," Cole said in a quiet voice. He then placed a cold, wet cloth on her forehead; that felt great. She appreciated what he was doing, and was so glad that she wasn't alone. Lucy watched as he walked around the bed and climbed in next to her. He found her hand under the blankets and squeezed it slightly.

"Just get some shut-eye, and don't worry about anything. Just get better soon," Cole told her. She fell into a deep sleep within minutes.

Lucy stirred as the light of the morning sun hit her face. She squinted when she first tried to open her eyes. She lifted her hand to shield her eyes. Lucy turned her head to look for Cole, but he wasn't in bed anymore. She could hear the water running in the bathroom. *He must be in the shower, getting ready for Troy's funeral.* Just the thought of Troy brought tears rolling down her cheeks. Lucy lifted herself on her elbows, trying to get up. However, when she did, the room started to spin. She flopped back down on her pillow as a rush of a cold sweat ran down her back. *How am I going to go to the funeral? I can't even sit up.*

Cole came out of the bathroom wearing a towel around his waist and smiled at her. He approached and sat down next to her on the edge of the bed. He reached over hand and brushed her cheek gently.

"How are you feeling? I hate to say it, but you still look pale. You should stay home and rest. Don't even think of moving from that bed. I'll be home from the funeral as soon as I can," he said.

"I'm so sorry. I really do want to go. I can barely lift my head from the pillow, though," Lucy answered. Her lip trembled, and a tear rolled down her cheek. Cole immediately wiped it away with his finger.

"Don't cry. It's not your fault that you're sick. I truly understand," Cole leaned forward and kissed her cheek. She felt sad.

"I'll make you some toast; it might help settle your stomach. Then I'll get ready," he told her, and walked away. Lucy could hear him in the kitchen as he fixed her something to eat. Within a few minutes, Cole was back with a tray that contained toast and a flat 7UP. He placed it on her night table. She didn't want to eat anything at the moment—or even look at it, afraid her stomach might reject it.

"Thank you, Babe, but right now I really can't even look at it. I think I'll stay in bed and maybe try to nap," she said. Lucy watched him open the closet to retrieve his uniform, which he had brought from his house the previous day. A feeling of dread invaded her heart, realizing Cole had to go to his best friend's funeral alone. She wouldn't be there to support him during one of the most important times of his life. He slipped on his pants and shirt, then carried his polished black boots to the end of the bed. He sat down and pulled one on, then the other. He bent down to tie them both. Tears began streaming down her cheeks at the thought he would be alone. She so wanted to be with him. *He needs me, and I can't soothe his sorrow.*

Cole turned his head toward her, and she saw the grimace of pain on his face. He reached over and took her hand in his, eyes fixed on hers. "Lucy, please don't cry. My heart breaks when you do. It will be fine. What's the matter?" he asked her in a soft voice. His hand came up and wiped the tears away.

"I feel so bad I can't help you, now that..." her words drifted off into a sob. His strong arms brought her against his chest. He stroked her hair to soothe her.

"Listen, Babe; I'll be all right. I know if you could be there, you would. You're sick, and that is nobody's fault. All I want is for you to get better. Now, please stop crying," he pleaded, and kissed her cheek. He pushed her back down on her pillow.

Cole stood up and took his jacket from the back of the chair to put it on. He picked up his hat and white gloves from the top of the bureau, ready to leave without her.

"You look handsome, Love," Lucy told him, giving him a small smile.

"I'll be back as soon as I can. Get better! I'll call when I can. Do you want me to leave King with you for company?" he asked.

Lucy shook her head. "Take him with you; I can barely get up," she answered. He blew her a kiss, and with a few long strides he had disappeared, King on his heels. She heard the front door shut. They were gone. She turned on her left side, fluffed her pillow and closed her eyes, trying to fall asleep again.

Chapter 17

Cole stepped outside on the porch with King by his side. He gripped the railing with both hands and bowed his head as apprehension about the funeral swept through him. His family had no choice other than to have the funeral at the largest facility in the area, because of all the officers and press that had converged on the area to attend the services. His heart bled for them, because he knew deep down they didn't want all this attention. They really just wanted to bury their son in a small church ceremony.

What he wouldn't give, to talk to his buddy one more time. A quiver passed down his back as he thought of how cruel Troy's death had been, how he'd died by himself. Cole had not been able to save him, and that would haunt him forever. He inhaled and exhaled several times as he tried to rein in his emotions and get going. The wind blew against his face as a memory of Troy came to mind, when he had come home from the shelter with King in his arms. King was just a puppy. *How Troy loved that dog!* He had cared for him when he had gotten hurt never leaving his side, and trained the dog over the years to become a K9 police dog.

King brought him back to reality when Cole heard him bark loudly. The dog was down by the porch skirt, digging a hole by the stairs. King was growling and howling. Cole stepped down the stairs and stood beside him. He laughed, because the dog was always digging holes everywhere. Cole grabbed the dog by the collar and pulled him back.

"King, be quiet. You're going to wake up Lucy, she's sick. Now, let's go," he said, yet the dog barked at him once again.

"Come on, boy! This isn't the time to dig holes. We have to get to the Civic Center," he told King. The dog looked up at him, but still barked and sniffed around the edge of the porch. Cole continued to walk toward his truck and opened the door for King. Cole stood to the side and yelled at him again.

"Come *on*, King. Let's go—now," Cole pointed at the back seat.

The dog finally obeyed him. He ran to the side of the truck, jumped up into the cab and sat in the passenger seat. Still agitated, King kept snarling under his breath.

"What's the matter with you today? Settle down. All right, let's get this over with." Cole started the engine and backed out of the driveway. He noticed King lay down on the seat beside him, but the dog was still restless. Cole drove the long lonely road in silence, holding the steering wheel tightly, trying to keep his feelings in check. This was the hardest thing he'd ever had to do in his life, burying his best friend. He was desperately trying not to cry or lose his composure as he approached the John Miller Civic Center. He was to meet up with the fellow officers who were pallbearers.

As he drove up, he could see Randall Avenue to his right. There were buses on both sides of the street; police officers were disembarking and making their way toward Houlton Community Park, where they were lining up for the ceremony. Two fire trucks parked parallel to each other near the entrance of the center, with their ladders raised and an American flag tied to them. It flapped in the wind, in between the ladders. Cole drove his truck to the specially designated area for the pallbearers. He hadn't made it to the wake to give Troy's mother and father his sympathies, because he knew he couldn't bear the hardship. He had also not wanted to leave Lucy alone while the search for Rodney was conducted near the house.

Cole shut off the engine and looked at the front doors of the arena. The commander and his subordinates dressed in their formal uniforms were swarming the entrance. The little thing that ripped into his heart was the black bands worn across his fellow officers' badges, signifying that one of them had fallen. Cole closed his eyes and sighed heavily. He quickly grabbed King's leash from the seat and attached it to his collar. One of the officers from the precinct was going to take King into the building, but he couldn't let him do it; Cole had to do it himself. Troy's best friends would have a last farewell together.

"Let's go, Boy," Cole said, and opened the door. He walked towards the building with his head held high. He clutched the dog's leash tightly as he approached the front entrance. Cole's heart pounded against his chest as he walked into the huge room. It was two hours away from the commencement of the ceremony, but people were already seated in the stands, waiting to give Troy their last respects, as due to a fallen officer. Cole walked up the main aisle to the front, where Troy's casket sat. A feeling of grief overpowered him. He abruptly stopped halfway, lifted his eyes and stared straight ahead. At the end of the aisle was a closed cedar coffin, draped in an American flag with a large bouquet of white roses resting on top. At both ends of the casket, two Maine State Troopers stood, holding the state flag. They were vigilant in honoring this fallen policeman. All around Troy's casket were baskets of colorful flowers from state officials and people who had known this great man.

Tears filled Cole's eyes from the pure love he had for this man. He looked down at King, sitting right next to his leg and glancing up at Cole, as if to say, "Let's go see him." Cole's whole body shook as he slowly took his first steps toward Troy for the last time. Within a few seconds, he was standing beside the casket. King walked over and sat near his master's coffin. It seemed the dog bowed his head in respect and Cole heard a whimper. Cole placed his hand on top of the dog's head and patted him. King lay down next to the coffin and laid his head between his paws.

"I know, Boy. I know; I loved him too," was all Cole could say. A chill passed through him. He shivered and another tear fell from his eye as he bowed his head. Cole stood there mentally talking to Troy for what seemed like an hour, but it was only a few minutes. He felt a gentle hand on his arm. Cole opened his eyes and saw it was his commander.

"Cole, it's time. We have to get ready for the ceremony," he said calmly, and let go of Cole's arm. Cole just nodded. He tapped his leg, and King stood up. He walked away with the commander beside him and King trailing behind.

***

138

Rodney awoke when he heard footsteps on the veranda. He didn't move except to grab his gun, laying beside him. Then he heard that fucking dog barking. Rodney tensed up, hoping he wouldn't be detected. He could see the dog's silhouette between the cracks of the porch skirt. The dog was digging a hole by the steps and barking. Rodney aimed his firearm at the dog, ready to shoot when he heard someone come down the steps. He held his gun firmly, still aimed where the dog was digging. His hands were sweating, and his heartbeat accelerated. *They're going to find my hideout. I'm not going down without a fight.*

Cole was talking to the dog, and suddenly the dog departed. Rodney cautiously crawled closer on hands and knees to look out through the crack. He laid his gun down on the ground next to him and started to bite his nails, which already had dried blood on them. They were raw, and his nervousness hadn't prevented him from sinking his teeth into his fingers. He watched as the dog jumped into the truck and they took off. Cole was all dressed up in his formal state trooper uniform. Rodney concluded he must be going to that other pig's funeral. He chuckled. *But where is Lucy?* He remembered Cole telling the dog to be quiet; she was sleeping. He glanced up over his head and stared at the hidden door. *She's alone and sleeping! Hmm! I wonder what she's wearing?* A sexual rush passed through him. He picked up the gun and put it in his pocket.

He slithered across the loose dirt until he was directly under the trap door. Rodney lifted himself to his knees and placed his ear to the door. He listened for any noise coming from above. Nothing but complete silence. He slowly pushed the door up a couple of inches, just enough so he could have a peek inside. It was still totally silent. He pushed it open wide, and like a mouse, he quietly leaped out. *I'm in her kitchen again, and she doesn't even know I'm here!* He was on his feet near the table in seconds. He took a few strides toward the bedroom, and listened for any movements. She must be deeply asleep. He continued until he was almost at the entrance of her room. He could see the frame at the foot of the bed. *I have to see her. I miss her so much.* Rodney took another step forward and heard a noise. He froze.

The floorboard under him had creaked from the weight of his body. He shifted his weight to the right and continued to advance until he was in the doorway. *Oh! My God! She is sleeping soundly, on her side. I can hear her breathing softly.* She wasn't entirely covered with the blanket. One bare leg rested on the edge of the mattress. He wondered how it would feel to touch her, and rubbed his hands together. His eyes were glued on her. He quietly took another step, stopped, and then stepped forward again, toward the bed. Rodney was soon standing at the foot of the bed. He tilted his head to the left, drooling on his shirt. He extended his arm, hand creeping closer to Lucy's leg. His fingers were inches from her skin. *What if she wakes up and sees me? I just want to feel a bit of her skin.* His fingertips lightly touched her ankle. *She's so velvety and delicate,* he thought. She stirred in her sleep. He watched as she turned over onto her other side and pulled her leg under the covers. He didn't run, or move at all. Rodney just stood there, content to watch her sleep. He licked the drool from his lips. He stood there immobile for about five minutes. *She belongs to me. She will be mine one day,* he thought over and over.

Finally, he took a few paces backward and turned around. He moved back to the kitchen out of her sight. He was about to return to his hiding place when he glanced at the refrigerator door. He opened the door, grabbed the cheese and salami, and shoved them in his pocket. Rodney reached for the loaf of bread. As he was about to pick it up, he accidently knocked a bottle of pickles onto the floor. He didn't move. He just spun his head in the direction of the bedroom. He heard her sweet voice coming from the bedroom. "Hon, is that you?"

He didn't answer. He just waited for her to come out and find him standing there. His eyes focused on her doorway. She never came. A minute passed. Rodney carefully lifted his foot away from the shattered glass with the bread in one hand, and took the few steps back to his hiding place. He bent down, dropped under the house, and closed the trap door without a sound, leaving the mess in Lucy's kitchen.

***

Lucy woke up an hour and a half later, feeling much better. She lay in bed, but had a weird sensation someone was watching her. "Was I dreaming, or did I sense someone in the house?" she asked herself. She listened to the sounds around her, not wanting to move from her spot. *I must be imagining things. It must be everything going on with the murder,* she thought. She shook her head.

What a stupid idea! She stretched her arms toward the ceiling and pushed the blanket away. Lucy sat up and grabbed her robe from the foot of the bed. She slipped it on, looking at her alarm clock. It was mid-afternoon. *Wonder when Cole will return. He shouldn't be much longer. He'll probably give me a call after the ceremony,* she thought.

She stood up and walked toward her small kitchen. She was hungry; maybe chicken soup would be good for her. She stopped in her tracks halfway there as she noticed a mess on the floor by the refrigerator. A jar of pickles had been broken on the floor. The juice and glass had splattered and scattered every-where, not to mention the small cucumbers all over the floor.

"Damn, Cole! You could have at least cleaned up your mess!" she exclaimed at the pickles on the floor. She picked up a roll of paper towels, bent down and wiped up the juice that was running all over the floor. Lucy cautiously gathered the broken glass, throwing it all into the wastebasket. She looked down at the floor after cleaning up the mess, and noticed particles of brown dirt around the table. She looked at the broom in the corner, but decided she would sweep it up after she ate something.

"When is this man ever going to learn to take his boots off?" she said out loud, a little irritated at Cole. She reached over and swung the cupboard door open, and saw the can of chicken noodle soup right in front. She opened it and poured it into a small pot on the stove. She waited patiently while it heated up, her stomach growling from hunger.

Finally, it was warm. Lucy gripped the handle of the pot tightly and poured the soup into a bowl. She brought it to the table and sat down, then spooned a tiny bit of the broth into her mouth to see if her stomach would reject it. But it seemed to accept it, so she continued eating it until it was all gone. Lucy felt much better after she had eaten. Her stomach was apparently settled, so she de-cided to take a shower. She put the bowl in the sink and turned around, headed for the bathroom to take a shower. She figured Cole should be back from the funeral soon, and he would need her.

She glanced out the living room window on her way, and noticed there were only a few officers left outside. She was glad they had moved away from her residence—but at the same time, she couldn't wait for them to apprehend Rodney. It made her jumpy that they still hadn't found him, after the extensive searches they had conducted. She bit her lower lip nervously and walked away from the window, feeling a bit sad that she couldn't attend Troy's ceremony.

Lucy opened the faucet in the shower and waited for it to warm up. She dropped her robe and gown to the floor then stepped under the hot water. Her body was sore, and her head still hurt a little. The water felt good as it washed away her pains. A few minutes later, she was done. She grabbed a large towel and wrapped it around her body. She stood in front of the mirror by the sink, her hair dripping. Her eyes had dark circles under them from being sick. Lucy felt another wave of sickness. She clutched her stomach with one hand, turning around quickly. She *just* made it to the wash bowl before she threw up all the soup she'd eaten earlier. She turned the faucet on, splashed cold water on her face and neck, then put her robe back on and returned to bed.

***

After the ceremony, Cole sat in his truck with his hands on the steering wheel and King by his side. He felt numb, shocked, and exhausted. His eyes just stared straight ahead at the people returning to their vehicles, but he didn't notice any of the faces.

It was early evening, and darkness had fallen; it was going to take him at least a couple of hours to get out of this traffic. It had taken all his strength to keep it together during the service, to not weep or break down. Suddenly tears ran down his cheeks. He put his hands over his face and sobbed one last time for his best friend. Cole felt like he couldn't breathe as he inhaled, trying to control his emotions. *How could this happen? Why did God take him away?* Cole thought. Finally his mind drifted to Lucy, and he didn't feel alone any longer. She was a great deal of comfort in his life, and he needed her by his side now more than ever. She would take his pain away, and together they would be able to move on. He wiped his eyes and decided to go find her as soon as he could. He glanced over at King. The dog was just sitting there quietly waiting, watching him.

"Let's go home," Cole said, and patted King on the head.

He slowly backed out of the parking lot, where thousands of people were lining up to move out onto the main road to return home. It would take him a while to get home—but he knew what was waiting for him, so it gave him hope. Cole drove home in silence for two hours. He finally arrived on the road to her house. He stopped at the checkpoint at the entrance of Lucy's driveway and rolled his window down.

"Hi, Cole. How was the ceremony?" the officer asked him politely.

"It was very sad. How's it going with the search?" Cole asked, changing the subject.

"So far, nothing. It's like he's a ghost," he answered, obviously disappointed.

"Don't worry. The day will come when we do catch him, and he will pay dearly," Cole told him, and rolled up his window. He couldn't wait to be near Lucy.

The officer just waved goodbye, and Cole continued up the road to the house. He turned off the engine, picked up his hat and gloves, and let King out of the truck. He walked over to the steps of the porch, with King trailing behind. He had just stopped to open the door when he heard King bark.

"Come on, Boy. Let's go see how Lucy is doing," he ordered—but the dog just sat there and kept on yelping. Cole watched as the dog started digging another hole near the veranda.

"Fine, have it your way; stay outside. I'll be back in a little while," Cole said. He went inside, closing the door behind him. He placed his things on the table, unbuttoned his jacket, and undid his tie. He threw it on the chair as he walked toward the bedroom to go find his love.

Chapter 18

Rodney lay on his belly in the dirt; his feet dug in against the wall farther from the skirt as sweat dripped down his brow. He watched that fucking dog come straight toward him when it jumped out of the truck. *They're back.* He heard Cole call the dog to try to get him into the cottage. Cole went inside without his mutt, though. Rodney looked past the animal and did not see any cops close to the house or in the vicinity. Only the wooden boards of the skirt kept him from being attacked again. It didn't look like King was giving up on him anytime soon. The dog didn't budge from the spot near the edge of the porch where he'd started scooping dirt away.

Rodney gripped his bow and an arrow carefully and tilted sideways, aiming at the ferocious dog digging a hole, again, exactly where he was hiding. He didn't want to use the handgun. It would be too noisy. He squirmed as far back as he could, to the wall of the foundation.

There was about thirty feet between him and the dog's position. He would only have seconds to shoot it, and only one shot before the dog was on top of him. Rodney knew he couldn't miss, otherwise he would be mauled by the dog again. Rodney also knew his hideaway would be compromised; he would quickly be discovered. He had nowhere to run this time. He still could feel the pain of the animal's last bite on his arm. He knew he needed to kill the dog before it got to him. He had shot a bow and arrow for years while hunting wildlife, but never this close. It was do or die.

Rodney held his bow steady, without shaking. His whole body vibrated inside from fright. He held his aim firmly as he saw the hole by the skirt getting bigger and deeper with every second. Dirt flew behind the dog as King snarled at him. Rodney could see his flashing teeth, and his head protruded under the skirt. *Get ready to shoot the second the dog's body comes under,* he thought. He held his arrow securely as he felt a rush of adrenaline. The dog's head was under the skirt, his paws clawing at the ground. *Wait for it, just a few more seconds.* Rodney held his breath, eyes focused on his aim. Rodney patiently waited. He saw the body of the beast come forward under the porch. *Shoot now!* The dog sprinted for him with his mouth open, his teeth bared and ready to attack. Rodney released the arrow; it flew from his bow in the direction of the animal.

***

Cole tiptoed his way through the kitchen to the entryway of the bedroom. He looked at his angel sleeping soundly, one arm under her pillow, and lying on her side. Her hair was spread across her pillow. He walked to the side of the bed and leaned down to kiss her gently on the forehead. Cole turned to walk away, although he really just wanted to crawl into bed with her and cuddle. He didn't want to wake her, though. He had just moved away when he heard movement behind him and a soft voice, "Hi, Babe. How are you doing?"

Cole pivoted on his heels. He was happy she was awake. He walked to the other side of the bed, undressed, then slid in next to her. He pulled her close, and she giggled. He immediately felt the warmth of her body against his. Her arms wrapped around his chest as she laid her sleepy head on his torso.

"Much better, now that I have you in my arms. How are you feeling? Better, I hope?" he asked as he held her close and kissed her head.

"Well, I woke up earlier and ate soup. I took a shower, but then I threw up again. I think the nap, and you being back, did me good. I feel much stronger," Lucy replied as she nuzzled closer to him.

"Good, I'm glad to hear it. Do you need anything?" Cole asked, still concerned. He brushed her hair away from her face.

"No, just you. How was the service? I'm really sorry I couldn't attend," she said sadly.

"It was really sad, and burying my best friend was the hardest thing I've ever had to do in my life. I hope I never have to experience anything like that again. I'm glad it's finished. I'm exhausted. I will always miss Troy. Right now, I just want to stay here in your arms and fall asleep next to you," he said. He closed his eyes. He inhaled her fragrance, smelling lavender from her hair.

"That's fine. I can do that all night. Sleep, and I'll hold you," she answered. He didn't say another word. She knew what to say to him to take his troubles away, and within minutes all his worries had faded. He was sound asleep.

Cole slept right through the night, never waking until the bright sunny rays hit his face in the early morning hours. Without opening his eyes, he could feel Lucy's body next to his. He was filled with contentment. He slowly opened his eyes and smiled to himself at how lucky he was to have found such a caring and loving woman. He listened to her breathe, and stared at her lovely face. He hated leaving her side to get ready for work. Cole slipped out of bed and headed toward the bathroom to take a shower. Afterward, he walked to the closet and got his clothes. He dressed for work carefully, trying to do it without making any noise. He'd put his pants on and was buttoning his inform shirt when Lucy spoke. "Good morning, Sweetie. Did you sleep well?"

"I slept like a baby. How are *you* feeling this morning?" Cole asked. He sat down on the edge of the bed next to her and bent over to tie the laces of his boots.

"How about I make you some breakfast before you leave? Are you hungry?" Lucy asked. She rubbed his lower back and watched his face. He picked up his belt from the bedpost; it still held his gun and handcuffs. He put it on as Lucy pushed the blankets away from her body.

"You sure you're up to it? I am famished," Cole said. He leaned and kissed her on the lips. When he pulled back, he whispered, "Maybe I'll just have *you* for breakfast." He heard her moan a bit. He massaged her thigh upward, then pulled her tightly against his upper body.

"And then you will be late for work—and still hungry," she teased. He let go of her and kissed her once more on the lips.

Cole stood up and paused as he watched her grab her robe from the end of the bed. She slipped it on and tied it at the waist. He walked to the kitchen, Lucy following closely behind him. He was headed toward the table down when he noticed the dirt on the floor near the table. He frowned, wondering how it got there, since he hadn't been near any dirt and neither had Lucy. He would have seen it, since it was such a large amount.

"You didn't go out last night, did you?" he casually asked, as Lucy was reaching into the refrigerator. She took out the eggs and placed them on the counter. She turned to face him with a puzzled expression.

"What are you talking about? I didn't leave the house," she answered. She continued to take things for breakfast from refrigerator and cupboards.

"Did anyone visit you while I was gone?" Cole asked. He bent down to examine the soil more closely, then stood up.

"No, I was in bed most of the evening. Why?" Lucy asked. She stopped scrambling the eggs and glanced up at him.

"The dirt on the floor over here," he said, pointing toward the floor. He suddenly spotted the trap door. He had never noticed it before now, probably because it was under the table. *The dirt... it had to come from the crawlspace. Could it be? Could Rodney have been hiding under the house all along? No one investigated that area! It never occurred to anyone. Oh my God! That was why they couldn't find him. Where is King? I didn't bring him in last night. I was so tired; I just forgot about him.* Cole looked around the room, hoping he was wrong, but King was nowhere to be found. Cole hadn't seen him since last night. He had been so consumed with the funeral he hadn't paid attention.

That's what King was trying to tell me yesterday, and I didn't listen. That's why he was barking and digging a hole. Rodney was under the fucking house all this time, he thought.

"Lucy! Lucy, come here!" he whispered urgently, and motioned for her to come to him. Cole's right hand reached for his gun. He pulled his Glock from its holster, and aimed the gun in the direction of the trap door.

"What?" she replied, unaware of what was going on until she glanced up at him. Lucy gasped. Her eyes bulged out and her hands started to shake. Her fright was apparent in her expression. She dropped the butter on the counter and froze. Her hands went up to cover the mouth when she saw Cole had his gun out. He signaled again for her to come to him. He placed his index finger on his mouth so she would keep quiet.

She scurried over and positioned herself behind him. He felt her trembling hand rest on his shoulder.

"What's going on?' she murmured in his ear. He never took his eyes off the trap door under the table.

"I think Rodney is hiding under the house," he told her in a whisper. He heard her make a small choking sound.

"I want you to leave the house, and run up the street to alert the troopers at the end of the driveway," he ordered her.

Lucy shook her head and squeezed his shoulder. "No, no way. I'm not leaving you. He won't harm you if I'm here. I'm staying–so just tell me what you want me to do," she said calmly.

"Okay. Quietly push the table to the side, then come back and stand behind me," he told her. Cole watched as she unhurriedly took the few strides to the table. She gripped the side of the table and pushed it away from the small door. Cole never budged from his spot, ready for anything. His adrenaline spiked at the thought of getting Rodney. His hand was firmly secured around the grip of his handgun, and his trigger finger was ready. Cole motioned Lucy to stand behind him, off to the side. He watched as she stepped to the far side of the kitchen. He saw tears building in her eyes.

He bent down and grasped the metal handle in his left hand. He pulled the door upward, swinging it open. He looked down into the darkness of the hole, ready for Rodney to jump out at him, but before he could do anything he saw the muzzle flash of a pistol. Three loud shots rang out from the darkness. Excruciating pain invaded his torso. Loud screams echoed in the room. Cole lost his grip on his gun, and his weapon fell to the floor. Cole felt his body being pushed backward. He hit the floor, then there was a total absence of light.

***

Lucy shrieked in horror when she heard the gunshots. She watched Cole fall backward onto his back as blood seeped down the left front side of his shirt. She jumped toward him, kneeling down beside his body. Tears streamed down her cheeks, as she sobbed hysterically. He was not responding to her. She grabbed a dishcloth from the edge of the counter and applied pressure on his wounds, trying to stop the blood flow.

"Cole! Babe! Oh, God, Cole. Hold on, Cole. I'll get help," she yelled. She heard a voice next to her. She whipped her head around and was face to face with the shooter. It was the man who had just harmed Cole; the man who had stalked her and eluded police these past few days; the monster who killed Troy, and now probably Cole as well. Rodney was standing in the opening of the trap door. He smiled at her with his yellow teeth. Nausea invaded her instantly; she was repulsed by the sight of him. Lucy could only see his upper body. His face and clothes were soiled with mud from being under the house, his hair matted with filth. She couldn't see his lower body; it was concealed by the floor. His dirty hand still held a gun pointed at Cole. *He shot Cole!*

"You're better off without him. I'm the one who loves you. It's my destiny to be with you," he said with a snarl. Rodney looked at her and grinned at Cole on the floor, bleeding. Her stalker jumped up and sat on the edge of the opening, his feet dangling below.

"You're fucking crazy. Stay away from me!" Lucy yelled at him. Anger filled her; then she looked down at Cole's limp body. She wanted to lunge at Rodney's throat and strangle him for what he had done to Cole, but she couldn't move. Her limbs were weak, and she thought she might faint. She fell backward on her heels, putting a hand out for support on the floor near Cole's body. A cold sweat ran down her spine. Her heart was racing from the events that had just happened. She could barely breathe, and kept trying to catch her breath as she pressed down on Cole's injuries. Her hands were shaking uncontrollably. *I need to get help for him. Otherwise, Cole will die just like Troy.* She saw Rodney swing his legs over the border of the opening and stand above them.

Rodney reached over and touched her hair. She pushed his hand away with a slap, trying to get him away from her. She could smell his detestable smell, and she wanted to throw up. He pulled his hand away for a moment. He just stood erect by her side and watched Lucy try to save Cole.

"Don't touch me," she screamed at him when she saw his hand lifting again. She swallowed hard, trying not to choke on her words. She would not give him the satisfaction of seeing how frightened she was feeling.

"I love you, Lucy. I can't live without you. Don't be afraid. I would never hurt you," he whispered. She wasn't listening to him. Suddenly there someone pounding on the front door and someone was yelling. She glanced over and could see the troopers through the window of her door. It was the state troopers who were guarding the house at the end of the road.

"Cole, is everything okay?" one of them asked, pounding on the front door. "We heard what sounded like gunshots."

"Help! Help! He shot Cole!" Lucy yelled with all her might. She heard a loud crash coming from the front of the house. The front door swung open, and the two troopers stood in the doorway with their guns drawn.

She felt a hand grab her arm tightly and yank her upright from the floor. Rodney positioned her body in front of him as a shield from the cops. She tried to break free, but his grip on her shoulder was firm. His gun was pointed close to her face.

She screamed, "Let me go!" She tried to squirm away from his grip, but he didn't listen. He held on to her tightly. She stared down at Cole's motionless body, horrified by the blood all over his shirt. *What if dies? Dear God, I can't live without him. I need you to help him,* she thought.

"Freeze! Police! Drop the gun and let her go *now*," one of the troopers shouted harshly at Rodney. The cops backed up a little and took cover on each side of the doorframe. She heard one of them call for backup on his radio.

"Stay away, or I'll kill her. I'm not afraid. I have nothing to lose. Leave, now," Rodney shouted. He dragged her backward toward the bedroom, his gun still pointed at her head.

"Leave us alone," he screamed at the cops. Tears streamed down her cheeks, and her heart was pounding hard against her chest. *Maybe if I kick him or elbow him he'll let me go; but am I taking a chance his gun might go off accidently? I could be shot, too.* She could smell his vile breath, he was so close to her. She could feel him rubbing against her, and she wanted to hurl. She couldn't stop the sobs, or the tears spilling from her eyes.

"Don't cry, Lucy! I would never hurt you. I'm just saying that so we can be left alone," he whispered next to her ear. He pulled her a few more strides backward to the doorway of the bedroom.

He screamed at them again. "Leave now, or I'll shoot her. I have nothing to lose." She stared at him. His sweating hands held her firmly across the chest. She watched in trepidation as the troopers backed away and closed the door.

"We'll be back," Lucy heard one yell. She was now alone with Rodney.

Chapter 19

Rodney watched the troopers retreat to the porch, and closed the door behind them. He sighed in relief. He loosened his grip on Lucy's shoulder and took a step back. She rushed toward the bed and sat down on the edge of it. He noticed her lip was trembling, and the tears hadn't stopped flowing down her cheeks. Her eyes were red and set on him, full of disgust. A feeling of sadness invaded him; she didn't love him, and she was terrified of him. A lump formed in his throat at the idea that she thought he might harm her. He loved her with all of his heart, and he couldn't imagine living without her. She was his life. *How can she not want me, now that the bastard who took her away from me is dead?*

He glanced at the dresser mirror. He looked dreadful. His hair was matted with dirt, his face was smeared with mud, and his clothes were filthy from lying in the grime underneath the house. He bowed his head, wishing he could clean up for her; but he couldn't, because it would give the cops the chance to arrest him. *Maybe if I tell her how I feel for her, it will help her understand, and she'll stop crying.* It broke his heart to see her so distressed. He approached the footboard of the bed, gun still in his hand. He watched as she pushed herself backward against the headboard of the bed.

"Lucy, I swear to you. I would never hurt you. I would die before letting anything happen to you. I love you too much for that," he told her in a soft voice as he stood near her.

"Don't come near me!" Lucy screamed. Her hands were raised in front of her as she moved away from him, to the other side of the bed.

"Please, don't push me away. You're my one true love. We can have a beautiful life together. We just need to find a way out of here. I love you, and I would do anything for you. My life is pointless without you by my side" he said, smiling at her, hoping she would realize how he felt.

"Stay away from me! You're crazy, and a murderer. I will never love you—*never*," she yelled at him, tears running down her face.

Rodney stood quietly, just staring at her, confused by her reaction. *She was always so nice to me before. Why did she change? What am I going to do now?* he thought. He walked to the window and closed the curtains while keeping an eye on Lucy. Rodney grabbed the chair from the corner of the room. He brought it near the doorway and flopped down on it. With the chair there, he could observe the door in the kitchen. He needed to decide what his next step would be. His leg started to bounce up and down. The tranquility of the room was eerie; the only sound was the soft sobbing coming from Lucy. Rodney turned to look at her again. She hadn't budged from her spot. She was a vision of beauty, even as upset as she was now. Her beautiful eyes were red from crying, and her face was wet from the tears. He sat motionless, watching her every little movement.

"Rodney, please let me go. I don't want you to get killed. The cops are not going to let you just walk out of here," she said. He didn't answer. He just continued to survey his surroundings trying to decide what to do. *I have to get out of here, but how? Should I take my love or leave her behind? Think! I can't live without her. Time is ticking away. I have to find a way out before reinforcements arrive, or I will definitely be trapped with absolutely no way out.* He bit his lower lip as he raked his dirty hand through his matted hair, trying to find a solution to his dilemma.

***

Cole felt a stabbing pain in his left shoulder when he came to. He grimaced from the discomfort. He slightly opened his eyes trying to orient himself. *Oh my God, Lucy!* He was overcome with fright for Lucy. *Where is she? Is she okay?* He barely moved his head, and he saw Rodney sitting by the bedroom door with Troy's gun in his hand. He didn't move a muscle. Cole was still dazed, and he tried to remember just what had transpired. He became immobile. He could see Lucy sitting on the bed in the background. She didn't seem to be hurt. *I have to find a way to help her.* He discreetly looked down at his left shoulder and saw that his shirt was red with blood. He was lying on the kitchen floor by the table. Rodney had shot him as he opened the trapped door. He felt the agonizing pain in his torso area. He wanted to lift his hand to touch his chest, but Rodney might detect his movement. *Play dead,* he thought. *You feel the pain, but you do have your bulletproof vest on. You'll be okay. You have to get to Lucy!*

He watched Rodney sitting on a chair at the entrance of the bedroom. He was about thirty feet away. Rodney was fidgeting in his chair now, staring beyond Cole toward the door. Lucy was alive, but very frightened. Cole closed his eyes, not wanting to attract attention. He had to figure out what to do. Otherwise, Rodney might shoot Lucy, too. *Where is my revolver? I need to find my revolver. I dropped it, but where the hell is it?*

Cole moved his head slightly, squinting, both eyes barely open in an attempt to locate his gun. *I see it!* It was about five feet from him, to his right by the chair. He couldn't grab it without being noticed by Rodney. He would have to wait. *Just be patient until Rodney stands up, or maybe walks away. He'll see you move and shoot you again–and he might shoot Lucy! Why is he sitting there? Why isn't he leaving? I can hear Lucy crying. How am I going to get to her? She's in his clutches! I have to rescue her!*

Think! The guys outside must have heard the gunshots when Rodney shot me. They must know he's in here, and that we're in here. I need to wait for the troopers to barge in to rescue Lucy. But I need to try to retrieve my gun. How can I alert Lucy? Maybe she can distract Rodney and get him away from the doorway. Cole lay on his back for what seemed a long time, eyes closed, immobile and listening for any movement. It had been no more than half an hour.

"I need to use the bathroom," he heard Lucy tell Rodney. He heard movement. He opened his eyes slightly and observed Rodney getting up from his chair and taking a few steps toward the bed to look at Lucy. Rodney seemed to be debating if he should let her go or not. He wiped his hand on the side of his pants.

"No problem. Go ahead, but don't try to escape. I'll be right behind you at the door," Rodney informed her. Lucy nodded and rose from her spot. She slowly passed by Rodney. Cole's eyes were glued on her as she came close to him. She stopped near him, tears rolling down her cheeks. She looked down at him, then he opened his eyes and winked at her. Her mouth opened, and her hand went up to cover it. She smiled down at him and glanced toward the bedroom. Rodney hadn't seen anything. Cole inclined his head toward his gun, which was by his side. She nodded once.

"I thought you needed to go to the bathroom. He's dead, so stop mourning over him. He never loved you like I do," Rodney told her. He took a step forward, gun in hand and waved for her to get going toward the bathroom.

Cole watched Rodney with both eyes barely open in an attempt to see what he was doing. Rodney just stood there, not moving, just staring at Lucy.

"Yes, I realize you're probably right. I'll be right back, after I wash my face. We'll talk," Lucy told Rodney. She continued to walk toward the bathroom. She opened the door and disappeared inside. Cole saw a grin appear on Rodney's face.

***

Lucy couldn't believe it; Cole was alive! Her heart was racing from delight as she closed the bathroom door. She stood with her back against the door for a moment. She wanted to jump up and down from joy. *I need to help Cole. I need to find a way to divert Rodney so Cole can reach his gun; or maybe I can grab it on my way out, if Rodney isn't watching me.* She looked down at her hands. They were trembling, but not from fright anymore—from excitement and hope. She reached over and turned on the cold water, filling her cupped hands with water. She splashed water on her face. It felt good and revived her. *Think! You have to find a way out of here, and rescue Cole.* She looked in the mirror and noticed her eyes were swollen and red from all the crying.

Lucy sighed heavily and stepped toward the door. She grabbed the knob and turned it slowly, without making any noise. She pulled the door open just a few inches, and peeked out into the kitchen area so she could see where Rodney was. He was nowhere to be seen. He wasn't at the doorway of the bedroom. He must be inside the bedroom. She scanned the floor and spotted the gun on the floor. She had to get to it.

She opened the door halfway then slipped out into the room, glanced at Cole on the floor and stepped lightly on the balls of her feet. She kept her eyes on the bedroom doorway. When she was near the pistol, Lucy slowly eased downward. With a sweeping motion of her right hand, Lucy grabbed the gun and tucked it into the pocket of her robe. At the same time, Cole tried to sit up with a grimace of pain. He held on to his chest with one hand, and extended the other toward her. "Give me the gun, hurry," he whispered.

Instead, Lucy ran to him, shaking her head. "I've got it. Let's get out of here before he sees us," she murmured.

She placed her arm around Cole's waist to help him up so they could escape. She lifted him upright with all her might. They turned around, rushing toward the kitchen door. They had only taken a few steps when Lucy heard Rodney's high-pitched, piercing voice. "NO! Stop or I'll shoot!" he screamed, at the top of his lungs.

Lucy and Cole froze on the spot. Her heart began to palpitate against her chest as a shiver ran down her entire body. She let go of Cole, who leaned on the table for support. She pivoted around him and stood in front of Cole to shield him from Rodney. She held her breath, afraid of what might happen. She looked into Rodney's eyes. She was petrified he would shoot Cole again, or her. She calmly placed her hands in her robe pockets to find Cole's gun. She gripped it and placed her index finger on the trigger, ready to defend them. Rodney stood in the bedroom doorway, feet apart. His brow was furrowed and his eyes glared daggers at Cole. He had a tick in his left cheek. He was holding the pistol in one hand; the other was balled into a tight fist.

"Rodney, I'm not going anywhere. I was just going to let him go outside, so he can get medical care. I've decided to stay with you. Just let him go," she lied. Lucy stepped forward, hoping Rodney would believe her, not kill her—or worst finish off Cole. She watched as his expression softened. Rodney tilted his head like a child would, appearing to be unsure if she was telling the truth.

"I've thought this situation over while I was in the bathroom. I never really loved Cole. He's like a brother to me, that's all. I realized you're the one I want to be with. Let him go, okay? And I'll be yours forever," Lucy said calmly. She smiled and walked toward Rodney. She was about ten feet from him. Lucy kept smiling; she needed him to trust her.

"You're lying to me. He must die so that we can be together," Rodney replied harshly, keeping his cold eyes on Cole. She glanced at Cole for a second then back to Rodney. Cole was holding on to the table with one bloody hand, the other on his chest. *He's near the door; if only he could open it, he would be safe,* Lucy thought.

She walked closer to Rodney, stopping to stand about a foot from him.

"Lucy, please don't," she heard Cole say. She didn't acknowledge him, afraid of what Rodney might do.

"Shut the fuck up or I'll kill you," Rodney told Cole angrily.

"No. Rodney, look at me. Look at me. Listen to me. I know how much you love me, now. Didn't I wear your wildflowers in my hair, when you brought them to me? Wasn't I always nice to you when you spoke to me? I'm right here for you," she said kindly. She took her free hand out of her robe pocket, and touched his arm lightly. He looked at her and smiled. Her mouth was as dry as sandpaper; her stomach was weak and upset. *Concentrate on him! I have to convince him to give me his gun.*

"You love me? Really? No lies. Tell me the truth," he said, barely audible. He raised his head and looked at her with tears in his eyes.

"Yes, I'll stay with you. Just give me the gun, and we can talk about it," Lucy replied. She reached out to touch his other arm.

He bowed his head low and said in a broken voice, tears streaming down his cheeks, "You don't love me. You love him. I'm no fool. You'll never love me like I love you. You just want me to give you my gun so you can be with him, Lucy. But I will always love you."

Without warning, Rodney raised the pistol. Lucy heard a sound like the cry of a wounded animal, and a gunshot rang out.

***

Cole lunged in the direction of the sound, agonizing pain throbbing through his shoulder. He could barely breathe from the discomfort of his wound. He was beside Lucy in an instant. He heard the door smashing open behind him, and the policemen screaming orders as they entered the room. Guns were drawn, pointing in their direction. Boots pounded hard on the floor as the officers approached them. Cole leaned down and wrapped his free arm around Lucy's waist. He pulled her close. Her whole body trembled as he held her tightly.

"It's okay, Babe. It's over. I'm here," he whispered in her ear, pulling her away from Rodney. Cole watched as a trooper kicked Rodney's gun away from his hand, to the far corner.

***

Rodney lay on the floor next to them, on his back in a pool of blood. Another cop rushed in to check for a pulse on his neck. Rodney's eyes were open, staring at the ceiling; he was not moving or responding. Rodney had shot himself in the temple. Lucy couldn't stop him.

Cole dragged her to the kitchen chair and sat her down. He removed the pistol from her pocket and placed it on the counter beside him. He then took his free hand and pushed her hair from her face as he looked in her eyes.

"Lucy, are you okay? It's over. It wasn't your fault. There was nothing you could have done to stop him. We're safe now. You were so brave," Cole told her. Cole feared that Lucy was going into shock. Lucy wrapped her arms around his shoulders and held him tight. He moaned as she held him, due to the pain from the gunshot wound. She pulled away and smiled at him. Cole picked up a wet towel from the counter and wiped Rodney's spattered blood from her face.

"I'm sorry. I'm okay now. You're the one who needs help. Let's get you some help," Lucy said and stood up. She took Cole's hand and started to lead him out of the house. Paramedics rushed inside to carry him to the nearest ambulance. Within minutes, an EMT was administrating medical assistance to Cole. At that moment, the commander of the SWAT team came to the ambulance door to talk to him.

"You're going to make it, Cole," he said and gave him the thumbs up.

"I think he'll be just fine, in time," the paramedic said, as he continued to check Cole's vitals.

"Cole, I just wanted to let you know we found your dog King by the side of the cottage. Rodney shot him with an arrow, in the shoulder. One of the officers took him to the veterinarian in town by squad car when we found him. I just received a call that he's going to be okay," he told him.

"Thanks, man, I owe you," Cole answered as he watched him walk away. Cole turned to look at Lucy, who was sitting by his side on the small bench in the back of the ambulance. He reached over and touched her knee. She covered his hand with hers. *Thank God! She's out of harm's way, and she is mine.*

"I love you so much," he told her. The pain medication took effect quickly, and he felt too drowsy to stay awake. He closed his eyes. She squeezed his hand, and just before he fell asleep, he heard his angel say, "*We* love you, more."

The End

About the Author

Ann El-Nemr lives in Shrewsbury, Massachusetts. She loves to travel the world and gets inspiration from all the different locations she visits. She has been an author for only a few years, but *Blinded by Obsession* is her fifth romantic suspense novel. Her other four novels in publication at the time of this writing are: *Betrayed, Forgiven, The Pledge* and *Lonesome Vagabond*. All her books were published by Jan-Carol Publishing, and are available on their website. She always loves to hear from her readers; you can contact her on Facebook, LinkedIn, or her website, www.annelnemr.com. She is always thrilled to chat with her fans.

www.ingramcontent.com/pod-product-compliance
Lightning Source LLC
Chambersburg PA
CBHW052137170626
46812CB00004B/1471